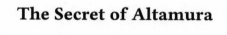

The Secret of Altamura

The Secret of Altamura

Nazi Crimes; Italian Treasure

Dick Rosano

Dedication

My career in writing would not have been possible without the love and support of my family – my wife Linda and daughter Kristen.

This book is dedicated to them, and to the people of the Mezzogiorno, including my own family, their traditions, their culture, and the aspirations for their children.

"The evil that men do lives after them;
...the good is oft interred with their bones."
William Shakespeare

Contents

Prologue

There was no simple way to hide the truth, yet there was no simple way to share it either, especially with people unprepared to hear the full story. For centuries, the people of Altamura had been strong enough to survive intruders from other countries – and their strength would protect them during this latest invasion of plunderers.

This book brings their secret to light, telling the world the truth of what lies beneath.

But some names must be omitted, because the truth could bring on damnation and ruin.

Chapter 1

A Hotel Room in Venice, May 2, 1943

Alessia stood before the mirror and carefully applied makeup to her cheeks, lips, and eyes. She was a master at it; not professionally trained, just naturally talented. Tonight this talent was especially important although her hands shook as she moved the brush across her face.

As she completed her task, a tiny tear escaped from the corner of her left eye and crept slowly down her face. Soon, her eyes started to swell as more tears came, but she fought the urge to surrender and turned her attention back to the work of making her face one that turned heads in Venice.

Once finished, she faced the bed and pulled the wrinkled sheets up one by one. Her hands trembled a bit as she tied the ends of the sheets together. So Alessia worked slowly, carefully, checking to make sure the knots were strong enough to hold her weight.

Tears fell on her hands and the bedding, tears blackened by her mascara, an unnecessary flourish for a woman blessed with youth and natural beauty. Her thoughts were focused on her affair with a German officer, Anselm. He was powerful and persuasive, and she might have fallen for him anyway, but she had surrendered to him out of fear. Anselm was generous with treasures he'd taken from Venetian homes and churches. But his jewelry and other gifts only made her feel like a whore.

"He betrays me, sleeps with other women, and pillages my country. I should get my revenge," she thought, conjuring up images of gothic mutilations. But her thirst for vengeance was not strong enough.

Tugging one more time on each of the knots, Alessia then tied one end of the sheets to the leg of the bed. Fearing that her weight would drag the furniture across the floor and swing her side to side below the ledge, she moved the bed up against the wall under the window, nudging its feet against the massive shoe molding of the ancient hotel.

She opened the window, pushed the shutters aside, and looked down into the canal below. The moon shined bright in a cloudless sky, and the brisk night air was refreshing, although its touch chilled Alessia's skin. Bells rang softly in the distance, some from churches, some from small boats passing in the night. A gentle mist hugged the water and spread over the channel below.

Alessia studied her city's panorama and peered beyond this canal into the labyrinth of those beyond. It was a scene familiar to her since childhood, but tonight she smiled only irreverently.

"Well, if the knots don't hold, I'll go for a swim instead."

Alessia sat on the windowsill and swung her legs over the edge. The mist tickled her bare feet and raised bumps on her arms. Once more, she tested the strength of the knot, then tied the sheet around her neck. Resting her palms on the stone ridge and giving a determined push, she sailed past the ledge and into the air. The sheets quickly drew taut, and by the time her body hit the hotel wall, her neck was already broken.

Alessia did not go for a swim that night.

Chapter 2

Piazza San Marco, Venice, May 3, 1943

Colonel Anselm Bernhard stood in the piazza in front of the gaping doors of the basilica. His hands rolled into fists rested lightly on the leather belt of his uniform. His short-cropped blond hair, clean shaven face, and icy blue eyes topped a muscular and athletic body.

Bernhard's stance and posture reflected the imperialism that his government wanted to impose on the world. He wore his uniform with pride; the razor sharp creases in his pants and the stiff material of the jacket signaled his exceptionality. That image was important for him to display to the soldiers in his command but also to the people of the cities and towns he laid siege to.

Facing the stone edifice of the Basilica di San Marco, Bernhard was clearly enjoying his latest conquest. The mist from the night before had cleared, leaving cool, crisp air on a pleasantly limpid morning. The colonel nodded his head at the basilica, as if he were engaging the great church in a silent conversation, when a young German officer walked up behind him.

"Sir, excuse me, but I have news you will want to hear... before others hear it, no doubt."

"Did you know, Hilgendorf," said Bernhard, "that Napoleon conquered this city?" Ignoring the young officer, he remained fixated on the glit-

tering façade of the Basilica di San Marco. "He stole vast art collections from the weak Italians groveling at his feet, even these," as he pointed up to the magnificent bronze horses at the apex of the church's entrance.

"He stole the horses of St. Mark's and sent them to his native Paris with the rest of the booty he had captured from conquered lands - - just as the soldiers of the Third Reich will do today, to glorify the German Empire."

Hilgendorf knew about Napoleon's theft of the horses. He also knew that Italy had recovered them from France and that Napoleon was not a native Parisian but was born and raised in Corsica.

The lieutenant, who knew his commander's moods, saw that Bernhard was reveling in fantasies of his own glorification, so correcting his historical musings would be unwise. Hilgendorf was well trained and knew that, in the German army, commanders like Bernhard were rewarded for being ruthless and uncompromising, so contradicting the decorated war veteran's grasp of history would be risky.

Hilgendorf, though an underling, had achieved a high level of education before entering service to the Third Reich in 1939 and he had mastered several foreign languages in the process. The superior officer standing before him had several times dismissed this accomplishment.

"Only German will be necessary in the future," Bernhard was quick to remind him.

The young lieutenant was taller and leaner than his muscular colonel and kept his light brown hair long enough to comb across the tops of his ears. He had romantic dreams of someday winning a beautiful bride, and in his youth had followed current fashions. Although now he maintained the clean shaven look German commanders encouraged, he still could have passed for a university student.

After a few more moments studying the bronze horses, Bernhard turned his head slowly and caught the young officer's eye. The colonel was not accustomed to being approached with an announcement that sounded like a warning.

"Well?" he asked.

"Alessia was found this morning hanging by her neck outside the hotel. She was dangling from the window, tied to a series of knotted sheets."

Hilgendorf paused to give his superior time to digest the news but, seeing no reaction, he continued.

"She was hoisted back into the room, her face was blue, and it was obvious that her neck was broken."

Still no reaction. Hilgendorf wondered whether Bernhard's slow response reflected some concern.

"What would you like me to do, sir?"

"Do?" Bernhard uttered matter-of-factly. "What should we do when some stupid girl hangs herself? What business is it of mine?"

The young officer turned to leave, but then halted at the sound of his name.

"Hilgendorf," Bernhard called out. "Go to her room and retrieve the gold necklace with the sapphires."

After the young officer departed, the older man took an elegant black leather notebook from his uniform pocket, opened it to a marked page and made some notes. Then he slipped the notebook back into his pocket and returned to gaze on the magnificent basilica, a symbol of the city he had just occupied for the Third Reich.

Chapter 3

Doge's Palace, Venice, May 5, 1943

Two days after Alessia's suicide, Anselm Bernhard was in his office, leaning over an ornate 16th century desk that once belonged to a Venetian Doge, the chief magistrate of Venice. He held the glass shaft of a pen lightly in his right hand, absent-mindedly pointing it at the official documents arranged carefully on the surface of the desk. With a clear conscience, Bernhard embraced the theory of Arian supremacy because it suited his own personal desires. The Nazi regime's plans to conquer Europe included a loose alliance with Italy, and these same plans allowed him to use his position of influence to plunder the riches of the land.

The leaders of the two countries, Adolph Hitler and Benito Mussolini, maintained a fragile relationship; but for the Führer it was only a charade. The privileges allowed the Italian Prime Minister were closely controlled by the Third Reich; the Italian people were not as easily smitten by the German dynastic plans.

But the coalition agreement carved out between Hitler and Mussolini created openings for German opportunists like Bernhard to take advantage of the relationship. With the presumed idea of supremacy, they could take what they wanted and justify it as "saving the disorderly Italians from themselves," a comment that Bernhard would make frequently in front of his troops.

The Nazi officer paused in his study of the war communiqués before him. He stood up, peered out the window, and straightened his shoulders in an unconscious throwback to the lessons pounded into the unconscious memories of the German officer corps. His posture was erect; his expression steely; and his uniform was starched, snug, and adorned with an array of ribbons carefully positioned above both pockets of the jacket. His appearance underscored his conviction that Hitler was lucky to have him.

Bernhard never doubted his own superiority, and he offered little loyalty to the general cause of the Third Reich. He considered Hitler violent, mean-spirited and dangerously unpredictable with an inferiority complex that fed his erratic behavior. Bernhard had heard that the Führer could pin a medal on a soldier's chest one day and order him shot the next, if he even vaguely suspected disloyalty.

"Killing Jews?" Bernhard thought. "Simple stuff for a madman." As for Hitler's "final solution" to exterminate the Jews, Bernhard had no opinion. The colonel frankly didn't care if people died, even the innocent ones as long as he wasn't expected to do the killing.

Art, money, and women were far more important to him. He could steal the art and money, and was willing to use his power to force the women into his bedroom. Given his personal agenda, his current position within the German power structure was perfect. He was assigned to confiscate artworks and other precious collectibles in Italy's private homes, churches, and museums, and ship them back to Berlin where they would be safely kept from "the disorderly Italians."

At first, the assignment was simple enough. With the execution or forced exile of anyone opposed to the Third Reich, the only complication Bernhard encountered was his own greed. Giving all the art to the German regime seemed like such a waste. So, he unofficially modified his orders, judiciously setting aside a portion of the plunder for his own "safekeeping."

The best of the art would adorn his private villa at the end of the war; some would be traded for the favors of the beautiful young Italian women who were brought to his quarters. And the remainder would be sent to

Berlin – enough to convince his superiors to keep him in charge of this mission to search and seize Italy's wealth.

Bernhard's attention returned to the matters on the desk, his reveries interrupted by the sight of the black leather journal that sat among the papers. He had confiscated it from a shop in Venice, a city famous for such things. He lifted it in his left hand, turned the pages to an unused page, and inscribed some notes in penmanship that was a tribute to his fine education. The swirls, slants, and ascending strokes would have made a medieval scribe jealous.

Bernhard had taken a moment to pause and read back his latest entry when he noticed Hilgendorf standing in the doorway.

"Why didn't you say something?" said Bernhard, as usual treating his deputy with more tolerance than he did the other twelve men in his detachment.

"My apologies, Colonel. I didn't want to interrupt you."

"Oh, it's nothing," Bernhard replied, tossing the glass pen on the desk but carefully closing the journal and slipping it into his pocket.

Hilgendorf was not allowed to read the journal, but he was perceptive enough to know what it contained. He knew that Bernhard spent more time writing in it when he had acquired a new work of art or plundered another church, so he surmised the colonel must be keeping an inventory of the booty and how he came to possess it. The only other activity that Bernhard appeared to document was his liaisons with the women he either seduced or coerced. The lieutenant knew that Bernhard liked to keep notes on his women since he sometimes consulted the journal when boasting of what he considered a lady's finer attributes.

When Bernhard once described a woman as "a work of art," the phrase convinced the younger officer that the colonel's other notes in the journal were reserved for the masterpieces he had stolen.

Bernhard was seldom interested in anything that Hilgendorf had to say. The young man, in turn, usually reported to his superior officer only when there was some official business to discuss. The colonel was growing less interested in the movement of troops, the success of the Nazi invasion of European countries, and the progress of Hitler's final solution. So before

Hilgendorf could explain the reason for his visit, Bernhard decided to set the direction for the conversation.

"Did you know that during medieval times, the leaders of this fair city stole the bones of saints? Venice, spectacular though it is, centered its efforts on collecting relics from dead Christians – bones, hair, and the like, to attract God-fearing pilgrims."

Hilgendorf knew some of this, but remained silent, knowing that Bernhard would prefer to deliver the lecture himself.

Standing up and stepping around the desk, Bernhard continued.

"I don't know who was more dim-witted," he smirked, "the collectors of these shards of anatomy, or the dullards who thought possessing them could bring everlasting life.

Once Bernhard finished his soliloquy, he fell silent, ready now to learn the purpose of his junior officer's visit.

"Commander Bragen has ordered that we hold the detachment here, or go no further south than Rome at this point."

The colonel considered the instructions, rubbed his chin, then turned back to his desk.

"Why is that?" he asked.

"There's more fighting in the south, and Bragen thinks that you don't like the battlefield."

Hilgendorf lowered his eyes, knowing that reporting a perceived weakness of Bernhard's was risky.

"I'm fine with fighting," the colonel replied stiffly, unable or unwilling to look his inferior in the eye. Bernhard shifted in his stance, and a random hand wave signaled his reluctance to take this conversation further.

"But I see no reason to risk our lives for a battle that others can wage. Our job is to preserve the art works of this great culture for the Third Reich." His sarcasm was not lost on Hilgendorf who knew Bernhard's selfish aims too well to believe that last phrase.

"We'll head south toward Rome, through Perugia where Etruscan treasures abound, and collect what we can along the way. Prepare a communiqué to the Berlin office informing them of our plans."

Hilgendorf snapped his heels together and saluted "Heil Hitler." Bernhard returned the salute absent-mindedly and ignored the lieutenant as he left the room.

Chapter 4

The Outskirts of Rome, June 2, 1943

The villa Colonel Bernhard had commandeered for himself and his men was on a hill in the outskirts of Rome. It was a magnificent structure, which the German officer thought he was entitled to, with broad terraces looking across the narrow valley that separated the estate from the buzz of life in the Eternal City.

The terrace that fronted the best view had with a stone portico, supported by great columns made of Carrara marble. A long wooden table and a dozen chairs served Bernhard when he desired to entertain his troops. This night he did, to celebrate the day's capture of this splendid villa and to allow the men the opportunity to remind the colonel of how popular he was among them.

But the meal would have been incomplete without a bevy of young Italian women who cooked and served it. Not all these beauties would be handed to his men. Bernhard planned to choose his own, but he wouldn't mind if arrangements were made for some of the others to entertain his troops when dinner was over.

Food was becoming scarce as the war raged on, and the women chosen to serve the German detachment knew this from personal experience. Bernhard pressed them to find ample servings for his men, a requirement that reminded the women of their own privation.

Numerous magnums of wine and platters of marinated vegetables from the local gardens began the feast. The young women, like most Italian girls, learned to cook from childhood and were skilled in the dishes of Lazio. In this case, they were also supported by less lovely elders relegated to kitchen tasks.

The evening began with bruschetta topped with fresh chopped tomatoes and slivers of red onion marinated in oil and herbs, a type of calzone colloquially called calascioni that was stuffed with ricotta, and a fried cheese side dish called provatura fritta. Filone, a regional bread that is a specialty in the environs of Rome, was used to sop up the juices of these dishes and soak up the prodigious quantities of wine the men consumed.

Next came carbonara, a plebian dish with exalted flavors of pancetta, cheese, and egg, and was met with inebriated cheers around the table. A platter bearing garofalato, a richly seasoned pork roast scented with local herbs and garlic, was carried out to the table by the women. The scent of stewed onions, carrots, cloves and tomatoes was met with howls of approval from the now over-stuffed diners.

As the food sated their palates and the wine loosened their tongues, the soldiers became more demanding of the women's attentions, some drawing the young ladies onto their laps and others leering intently at the scooping necklines of the well-proportioned waitresses.

"Now you know," said Bernhard, standing at the head of the table with a large wine glass in his right hand, "why the Romans were so fond of bacchanals." With that ill-reasoned play to history, the colonel poured a healthy gulp of the red liquid down his throat, swallowed hard, and wrapped his left arm around the comely lady by his side. She smiled wanly, knowing what was in store for her, but careful not to resist in front of the lesser officers. Such behavior could draw unwanted ire from the man who seemed to think she belonged to him.

As the evening wore on, the wine took its toll on the men. Some forced themselves on the women, while others retained some civility despite their drunkenness. In ones and two, the crowd around the table departed, leaving Bernhard and his chosen companion last of all.

The colonel was not a brute, but he also did not consider letting the ladies in his company decide the course of events. He maintained a certain high-minded behavior, convinced that his superior bearing would impress any female in his presence, but he would nevertheless resort to power to command what he wanted.

This evening he was especially gracious. Perhaps it was the spectacular summer evening outside one of the world's greatest cities. Perhaps it was the wine. Most likely he was simply too consumed by his own sense of importance to let the moment descend rapidly into tawdry action.

Bernhard stood at the edge of the terrazza with glass in hand, gazing across the valley to the lights of Rome. The young lady – whose name he hadn't even bothered to learn – strode up to his side. She was afraid of the man, but also curious. The German officer had a bit of class, and she knew that in wartime she could do worse.

She slipped her arm into his and looked up into his eyes. Bernhard continued staring down on the city, but after several minutes drained the last of the wine and turned toward her. With a possessive smile, he wordlessly showed her that he was in command. She was now his prisoner of war.

Chapter 5

St. Ambrose Church, St. Louis, Present Day

Carlo DeVito had spent his entire life in the suburbs of St. Louis. "The Hill," to be exact, the neighborhood with a concentration of Italian-American families whose traditions and culture harkened back to the world of southern Italy.

His family was certainly Americanized, but some habits remained. His father made his own wine together with other families on The Hill, and his mother preferred to fill her ample dinner table with dishes that were based on Italian ingredients and recipes. But Carlo had been born in America, just like his brother and sister, and he clung to the culture and habits of those less-Italian classmates of his.

Still, the challenge of reconciling his native culture with America remained an intrigue for him. He was quieter and a more pensive than his siblings when he surveyed the gathered clan at the clamorous evening meals. He laughed hearing the old stories and familiar jokes of the uncles, and he tolerated the cheek-pinching of the aunts, but Carlo also wondered what were the essential ingredients of a real Italian family.

Food, certainly; wine, music, and close family. These were all parts of the tapestry of life, and Carlo was thankful to have them all in his. He knew that his experience of growing up differed from many of his friends, and he wanted to be able to express it. But before he could express it, he needed to understand it better.

Carlo had decided to take a semester off from classes at Washington University in St. Louis. He would spend a month in southern Italy, staying with a family known to his own, and he would absorb what he could of the "Italianisma," transforming his understanding of culture and – hopefully – coming home with a deeper comprehension of what it meant to be Italian. And with a better awareness of what his parents and uncles and aunts meant when they talked about the "Old Country."

On the morning of his departure, Carlo returned to the church where he was baptized and confirmed, and where he assumed he would one day be married before repeating the cycle with his own children. St. Ambrose was his parish church, but it was also his refuge. He didn't feel particularly religious for most of his young life, but he found that the somber silence of the chapel on Wilson Avenue gave him time to reflect on who he was, what he wanted, and how might a greater power be involved in deciding these matters.

Just before eight in the morning he slipped through the heavy doors at the entrance and walked up a few rows of pews before choosing a spot that seemed right. Which row to sit in was a spontaneous decision, one Carlo made every time he was in church. Too far back and it felt like he was avoiding contact with God; too far forward and he felt like a sinner begging forgiveness. So he would let his mind wander and let his feet decide where he would settle, like a divining rod seeking water.

This morning, he leaned against the cool wood of the seat, rested his hands on his knees, and stared at the image of the crucified Christ above the altar. The carved face looked pained, twisted by fever and mortal injury.

Carlo's gaze swept the chapel. He had been an altar boy at this church and knew its nooks and crannies well. He knew that the entrance to the priest's sacristy was on the right, that the sign noting the day's hymns was beside the altar, and that the tabernacle used in the Holy Mass was kept locked.

Carlo also knew that a small bone fragment from the body of St. Ambrose was kept in a reliquary on the right side of the chapel. It was a mere sliver of something that wouldn't be recognizable as human except by a trained scientific eye, but the Vatican had assured the diocese of its authenticity.

It was the most cherished relic in the Church of St. Ambrose, although most of the parishioners had long since forgotten its presence in their midst.

After a half hour of deep contemplation, Carlo made the sign of the cross, stood up and walked to the exit, planning to be back at his apartment in plenty of time before his sister and brother arrived to take him to the airport.

Chapter 6

Berlin, Present Day

The young art collector was pacing the floor in the grandiose antechamber to the museum curator's office. Martin Bernhard was uncertain what to say or even think, but he needed time to explain once and for all to his boss, the curator, why he had been making so many trips to Italy.

Martin was a product of the new generation of Germans who embraced a more modest style and peaceful temperament. It was as if this evolution of the national personality was part of the restructuring of the national psyche after the Second World War. His friends wouldn't describe Martin as shy, but he was quiet and thoughtful, traits that made some people mistakenly conclude that he lacked depth.

Standing just under six feet tall with short cropped hair and blue eyes, Martin was the epitome of the new German society. His university education fitted him well for a successful career, and his dedication to art restoration brought him confidence in the cause and a sense of personal worth in his pursuit.

Martin pursued his love of the Renaissance masters with a passion ever since his graduation from the university where he has studied art history. His grandfather, Anselm Bernhard, may have planted the seed of the passion Martin showed for art. Family stories of the old German suggested that he was also an art lover and his grandson was familiar with tales of the masterpieces that adorned the museums of the world.

Martin was tall, but his wife, Margrit, constantly reminded him that bending over old paintings while peering through a magnifying glass would turn him into a crook-spined old man. Martin laughed at her but gave her an unmistakable look of love as he cocked his head to the side when she upbraided him so. Margrit was his greatest treasure. After dating so many young ladies in his youth, he knew she was the only one for him.

He was in love with Margrit, but he was also in love with art. No detail escaped his attention, and his professors marked him as someone who would achieve great success in the field. But Martin's attention had turned to darker thoughts after his grandmother died, the precise moment when she revealed a secret to Martin that would change his behavior forever. The change was not evident to those around him – he hid the tension well – but he knew that the news he received from her on her deathbed would alter the direction of his life.

Martin paced the antechamber waiting for Professor Gustave, a man who had been a great mentor for Martin and encouraged his research into the art works of Italy from the Renaissance onward. He had never questioned Martin's requests to return again and again to the country of da Vinci, Michelangelo, Rafael, and so many other masters over the past three years. Gustave considered Martin's contributions to the museum – and to his own understanding of the Renaissance – as ample payment for the young man's visits to the peninsula from their headquarters in Berlin.

Gustave himself had a broader interest, focusing on the art works that emerged from churches liberated from the dark times of the Middle Ages. He found the primitive nature of some of the work to be revelatory, as if while staring at the paintings he could slip into the minds of the people who lived during that time and imagine their struggles, their fears, and their hopes.

The curator was older now, and less likely to travel, but he encouraged Martin's pursuit of art and knowledge. However, even with his mentor's support, Martin was still concerned about explaining to his superior what he was doing. It would not hurt the museum; of course, it was personal. Still, Martin was loathe to admit to Professor Gustave what his family had done.

The older man swung open the door to his office and welcomed Martin in. Gustave and his generation bridged the gap between Germany's war years and the present, and his appearance reflected this cultural evolution. Although he wore the rumpled shirt of a university scholar, he entered the room with an erect posture that bore witness to the presumed greatness of his race.

The men sat at the table in the center of the room where coffee cups and Danish had been set out, and exchanged light greetings. They discussed the heat spell sweeping through Germany at the moment and other small news of the present.

"I've been busy lately with my grandchildren," Gustave offered with a little smile. "They have more energy than an old art collector has."

Gustave didn't notice Martin's mood, or give any indication of the level of concern that Martin brought into the room. After two sips of coffee and more light conversation, Martin looked down at the table and resisted the standard replies. Gustave tried once more to establish a familiar banter that usually occupied their meetings.

"Did you know that my Eva..." but Martin interrupted him.

"You know I have been spending a lot of time in Italy, sir." Gustave nodded assent.

Taking a deep breath, Martin continued.

"Well, I believe it's time that I told you more about my activities, and shared more with you than I have so far.

"My grandfather," Martin stammered, then paused.

"Umm, I mean my grandmother," pausing again, now at a loss for words. Martin's right hand went to his tie knot, drawing it a bit tighter against his neck.

Gustave patiently regarded the young man, his eyes full of concern, but he allowed Martin to take his time and begin when and where he wanted to.

Finally, Martin said, "A few years ago, I sat with my grandmother in her home. She was old and frail, but her mind was sharp and her memory even sharper.

"She told me stories about my grandfather that I had not heard before. Instead of stories of a brave officer's career spent struggling in a reprehensible military culture of world war, she told me secrets about my grandfather's life that had been kept from everyone in our family.

"Anselm Bernhard was a colonel in the German army, a member of the Nazi party, but a somewhat unwilling participant in those wartime atrocities that we all abhor now. It is true that he didn't engage in any of the war crimes that have been recorded, and my grandmother swore to me that this history is correct as it stands. But she also told me about his personal behavior – things that I never knew.

"Anselm Bernhard loved great art. He knew it well," Martin continued, "of course, not as a professional knows art, not like you, Professor. But he appreciated great art and was drawn to the treasures of Italy during the war."

At this point, Martin paused, taking a deep breath before continuing.

"My grandfather confiscated many works of art belonging to Italian museums, churches, and families in the name of the Third Reich."

Gustave fidgeted a bit at this news, knowing full well that the German military had stolen countless precious artworks during the war. Nothing could compare to the horrible brutality of the extermination camps, but the professor was personally repulsed by the theft of treasures that his countrymen had committed in the name of all Germany.

"He confiscated the art," Martin continued, choosing a more official word rather than 'stole.'

"He confiscated paintings and sculptures, sometimes even from private homes, and seized them for the German regime. But he..." and here Martin paused again, "...he kept many for himself. Some," Martin whispered confessionally, "he gave to women he seduced while occupying their towns."

Gustave was disappointed to learn about the young man's family history, but not surprised by the well-known crimes that had been committed in the name of Aryan supremacy.

"My grandmother gave me a journal that he left, a small leather-bound book in which he listed all his acquisitions. The journal describes the piece, the place where it once resided, and the day that he took possession of it. I have been working from this journal, piecing together my grandfather's movements, and attempting to locate each of the pieces that he stole, trying to find the rightful owners. Sometimes, the art belongs to a church and, if it wasn't bombed out during the war, I can return the work to the pastor. Sometimes, the art belongs to a family. That's the hardest part, because so many people were killed or uprooted during the war that it's harder to find them than it is to find the churches that he looted."

Martin's mind wandered back to more satisfying memories of the art pieces that he had found and returned. He had averted his eyes from the questioning looks on the faces of the young priests taking possession of the paintings and small sculptures, not wanting to let the guilt shine through his eyes.

"Sometimes the work of art wound up in another's possession where it has remained so long that it is nearly impossible – legally, anyway – to wrest it from its current holders." Martin and Gustave were both painfully aware of the long-running court battles fought by the victims of these crimes to regain personal possessions that had been taken by the Germans decades before.

Martin struggled most with this last category of theft, knowing that he had limited resources or legal power to return those to their rightful owners in Italy.

Gustave laid a hand on the young man's arm. "What can I do?"

"Nothing, sir. But I want to continue my quest, I want to make amends for my grandfather's sins, and find a way to return the art and other possessions that he stole from the Italian people."

"This was difficult for you to admit," Gustave assured his protégé, "and I'm sure even more difficult for you to live with. Go, Martin, find these great works, but keep me posted. Art is truly a world in itself, and finding great works that can be returned to their proper place does us all a service. We don't have to own the pieces ourselves."

Chapter 7

A Long Stressful Night

Martin drove the short distance through Berlin to his home. He pulled the car to the curb and parked, but sat for some time without exiting the vehicle. He reached into his briefcase and withdrew his grandfather's old journal, thumbing through the pages, glancing occasionally at the descriptions of the stolen art.

Then he flipped back in the book to the final pages that contained notes of a great treasure in southern Italy. Anselm Bernhardt had only rumors to go on, and the contents of the cache were not even well laid out, but the old colonel's desire poured forth from the words on the page. Martin stared long at the entries, wondering what his grandfather was after.

Finally, he put the journal back in the briefcase and stepped out of the car. Martin had already decided to talk to his wife about this tonight, as he had told his mentor at the museum. He didn't doubt Gustave's sincerity; the atrocities of the Nazi regime were facts the German people had dealt with for decades. They were ashamed of them, but also convinced the Third Reich didn't reflect the true German spirit.

Still, facing the sins of the past was not going to be easy. Martin was particularly upset that his country's disgrace was deeply linked to his own family. Now he had to raise this issue with his wife.

Margrit was the sweetest woman he had ever met. She possessed a simple charm and grace that drew him to her from their first date. She believed in the goodness of human beings and was the very antithesis of the evil spread by her countrymen during World War II. In fact, it was precisely this natural benevolence and good nature that would make it so difficult for Martin to tell her what his grandfather had done.

She knew that Martin's family had been heavily involved in the Third Reich. She also knew that Anselm had been a colonel in the Nazi army. But her knowledge of his life and career was limited to the colonel's assignment as an art expert, charged with collecting great art and protecting it from the ravages of the war.

Margrit hadn't been told that Anselm was a thief; that his requisition of great art was for felonious purposes, not protection; nor that he had deceived his superior officers by keeping many of the artworks for himself.

And she didn't know about Anselm's rape of Italian women or about the black leather book where he recorded the theft of Italian art as well as young women's honor.

As he walked slowly across the street and up the stairs to their apartment, Martin struggled with how to tell his wife about his family's past. She knew of his travels to Italy but only the same short version that Martin had given Gustave before that day, to explain the several trips to Italy over the preceding three years. Now that he had decided to clear the air with Margrit, ask her forgiveness for the deception, and hope that her goodness would prevail, he could only hope that she would understand and not conclude his grandfather's character flaws were part of his own makeup.

He reached for the doorknob of their apartment, turned it clockwise, and pushed the wooden door open. The aromas of the night's dinner enveloped him and, as he closed the door behind him, he heard the soft notes of Chopin's Sonata in B flat minor. Margrit liked to listen to the classics, Chopin most of all.

The aromas created by Margrit's cooking and the soft sounds created by Chopin soothed Martin's spirit for a moment. He greeted his wife with a kiss on the cheek and wrapped his arm around her waist while looking over her shoulder to see what was on the stove. Margrit smiled but then saw something in his eyes that troubled her.

"What's the matter, darling?" she asked.

Martin shrugged, content for the moment to put off the sordid conversation. He helped Margrit set the table and serve the food. After they both sat down at their little wooden dining table in the room, she stared expectantly at him while he poured the wine, but waited quietly until he offered the reason for his mood.

"I met with Professor Gustave today," he began. Martin stuck the tines of the fork into the food on his plate, stirred the peas around a bit, then continued.

"My grandfather, Anselm Bernhard, you know who he was?"

"Yes, of course. What about him?"

"My grandmother, his wife, gave me a journal that Anselm kept during the war."

"Okay, but she died three years ago. What does the journal say?"

"Anselm kept it as a diary of sorts. You know he collected art from around Italy during the war."

"To preserve it, right?" That was the story Margrit wanted to believe but she suddenly flushed and a sense of dread enveloped her.

"He wrote down all the works of art and other items he took from the Italian people. He stole those things, Margrit, he wasn't trying to protect them from the war."

She paused.

"Did he keep them?" she asked in a voice slightly above a whisper.

"What?"

"DID he keep them? The artworks?" she pressed.

"Yes, well no, not all of them. He kept some and sent truckloads to Berlin for the Führer, and the officers of the Third Reich."

Martin took a sip of wine and swallowed hard.

"My grandfather did not engage in any of the slaughter, but he is not blameless, either. My grandmother read his journal and learned there was more in there than just the description of stolen art. Included were references to women... women that he had affairs with while he was in Italy."

"He was having affairs? He was married to your grandmother at the time! He was unfaithful?"

Martin wished that he could call it 'just' adultery.

"These weren't exactly affairs," he began, taking a deep breath. "War is no excuse for what he did, but invading armies often abuse the victims of the invasion." He knew he was beating around the bush, so he tried again.

"Anselm Bernhard took the spoils of war, art and women, for his pleasure. He stole the art and forced the women to sleep with him."

Margrit stared at Martin, but he couldn't meet her eyes.

"I didn't know anything about this until just before Grandmother's death. She had the journal and she read through it, discovering the crimes her husband had committed. She kept his secret all these years but, when she was very sick, she told me about Anselm's conduct during the war.

"She said, 'Martin, I can't return what he stole from these women, but I want you to help me return the art he stole from their families.' She gave me the journal and told me to study it carefully. She wanted me to know about his debauchery. She wanted me to hate him. But Grandmother also said she wanted me to develop a firm resolve to repair what my grandfather had done to the people of Italy.

"For the last few years, on my trips to Italy, I have found some art and I have been able to uncover the church or, in some instances, the families that deserve to be compensated, and I have done so."

"Have you met any of the women?" Margrit asked. It was not an unexpected question, and Martin was prepared.

"No, I haven't looked for them. Such crimes cannot be wiped away by my actions. He is paying for them in hell."

"What are you going to do now?"

"I will return to Italy again. I have found notes in the back of the journal, oddly separated from the rest of the notes alluding to a great treasure that my grandfather hunted for, maybe never found – a cache of immense value hidden in a rocky plateau area called "the Murge" in the heel of Italy, near a town called Altamura."

"If he didn't find it, why must you look for it? It must be safe," Margrit said.

"Yes, probably, but his notes have raised my suspicions. Instead of a streaming narrative, the notes on the Murge are cryptic, drawings, and some writing in Latin, Italian, and even Hebrew. It's obvious that this held a special interest for the old bastard, and I want to be sure that he didn't find it and hide it somewhere."

"Are you sure you're not as obsessed as your grandfather?"

Magrit's question startled Martin, and he looked down at the napkin on his lap, somewhat embarrassed that his wife would cast doubt on him.

"Yes, I'm sure. But I want to find the treasure of the Murge nevertheless." And now even he doubted his motives.

With that, Martin rose and left the table, having barely eaten his dinner. Margrit knew her husband was a good man, and that he was grappling with this strange and troubling information, so she said no more.

He wandered off into the office at the back of the apartment, then stood by the window peering out into the darkness. Martin thought back to Margrit's words, about whether he was just as obsessed as Anselm about the treasure in southern Italy. He had been quick to respond; a delayed reply would have left his wife suspicious of his intentions, but Martin had more trouble denying it to himself.

Chapter 8

Bustling Through Da Vinci Airport, Rome

Carlo's return to life all'Italiana began at Rome's Da Vinci Airport. Also known locally as Fiumicino, it is a crossroad for both American and European travel, where the Old and New Worlds seem to greet and shake hands. The bustle of commerce, the jostling of foreign visitors, cigarette smoke mingling with perfume, espresso, and Italian food leaves an indelible impression on everyone who passes through its terminals. Arriving here on an international flight is almost like stepping out of a wormhole of time into a world that was at once mysterious and exotic, yet familiar and comforting.

On the tracks of the inter-city train that connected the airport with Rome itself, Carlo lifted his luggage onto the waiting car. The hiss of the train announced its intention to embark, as the wheels slowly creaked into motion. It was a calm twenty minute ride to Rome Termini, the train station that served as the hub for transportation into and around the city. Recovering his bags, Carlo disembarked from the car and walked toward the exterior of the public arrivals area. He stepped out onto the curb and gazed at the ancient buildings what circled the train station in a welcoming embrace.

Carlo took a moment to gather it all in. His last visit to Italy was four years earlier, but he still had powerful memories of the trip. Now, he couldn't resist smiling as he watched the people rushing by; listening to the distinct sounds of this ancient city that blended church bells, car horns, pop music, and police sirens; and he breathed in the scents of Italian urban life. The intimate words shared between a passing couple seemed to be whispers to Carlo himself, welcoming him back to a world that he knew was so different from his home in America.

After letting it all sink in, Carlo walked the few blocks to the hotel he had used during his latest stay, the Hotel Venezia on Via Varese.

In America, the streets around train stations are not always the most attractive. But in Italy, as in the rest of Europe, the neighborhoods surrounding these centers of transportation nearly pulsate with the melodies of daily life. So Carlo had chosen a hotel that was within walking distance to restaurants and commerce, dispensing with the need for a taxi.

Once he deposited his luggage in his hotel, Carlo washed up quickly in the hallway bathroom then, feeling suddenly rejuvenated, returned to the streets to soak in the atmosphere of Rome.

His hotel was only a short walk from the Coliseum, ground zero for ancient Roman life and, most definitely, for every one of Carlo's visits to the city. Tickets had been required for many years, a feeble attempt to control access and, thereby, limit pedestrian damage to the ancient site, but security had tightened since Carlo's last visit, including bag checks and posted guards, a fact he deeply regretted since he liked to begin his return to Italy with a thoughtful meditation on the upper deck of the amphitheater.

Higher ticket prices and longer lines due to security killed that thought, but Carlo shrugged it off. He would stay overnight before catching a train to the south, so he would have time to visit other favorite haunts in Rome that usually made up his itinerary. Some of it would be rushed, and he didn't want to feel cheated of the time he could spend, so he decided to limit his attention to only a few Roman landmarks that day.

He walked to a spot on a street above the Roman Forum that allowed an unfettered view of the ancient ruins below, and one that tour-book-toting tourists wouldn't discover on the pages of their guidebooks. He leaned against a crumbling stone wall and considered the ruined glory that stretched below him. Unlike the Coliseum, where events centered around gladiator battles and the slaying of prisoners and wild animals, the Forum was the center of government, politics, and commerce in ancient Rome. The buildings were gone, but many columns still remained along with the excavated footprint of great halls. From his lofty aerie, Carlo could easily make out the lanes and buildings that had once stood there.

After contemplating that – and his own great luck to be once again in the Eternal City – Carlo wandered off in search of wine and relaxation. He took the long way around, circling Piazza Venezia to get a view of the massive, early 20th century monument to Italy's first king, Vittorio Emanuele II, that the Romans know call the "wedding cake" because of its balanced proportions, gleaming white façade, and strict symmetry.

From there, Carlo passed through Piazza del Pantheon, smiling at the throngs of tourists who pushed through the doors of that venerable monument which for its 2,000 year history had variously served religious and public functions. The cafés that dotted this piazza were predictably filled with tourists. He continued on to his favorite spot in the city, Piazza Navona. That, too, was a magnet for tourists, but he couldn't resist its draw.

Carlo knew that drinks and light snacks were cheaper served to the people standing at the bar, but he was feeling a bit of jet lag and willing to pay a bit more to sit down. Finding an empty table at Café Bernini on this long, oval piazza, he took a seat and waited patiently for some attention from the wait staff. Italians are famous for being friendly and accommodating people, a well-earned reputation that waiters did not necessarily copy. Waiting at a table for service is a frequent problem, but it is an irritation only to those not expecting it. Carlo was prepared, so he sat relaxed and enjoyed the spectacle of Rome's daily life.

A few moments later, a waiter appeared.

"*Buon giorno*," he said curtly, tossing a cocktail napkin on the table.

"Campari and soda," Carlo said, realizing too late that he resorted to English, but knowing the waiter would understand.

"*Subito,*" said the man, spinning on his heel and retreating to the interior of the café.

Then, just as quickly, he returned with a short tumbler of red liquid and a slice of orange. A little bowl of marinated olives completed the order and Carlo settled down to one of his favorite treats in Italy: an afternoon of sunshine, a chilled Campari, and Italy's native fruit – the olive – all complemented by the sights and sounds of the Romani in the piazza.

After a short while and another Campari and soda, Carlo reluctantly gave up his seat. He knew that he needed a bit more time in the hotel to clean up and thought a brief nap before dinner would be therapeutic.

Chapter 9

Allied Forces Invade Sicily, July 1943

Hell came to North Africa in June of 1940 when Mussolini declared war on the colonial governments there. The battles were fought mainly in Libya, Tunisia, and parts of Egypt. This was prior to the United States entering the war, so the British were left practically alone to fight the Italian army in a see-saw war that had battlefields and cities changing hands several times over a three-year period.

In the months bridging late-1940 and early-1941, mounting losses suffered by the Italian army presaged a decline of Mussolini's campaign in North Africa. So Germany dispatched Field Marshall Erwin Rommel and his Afrika Korps to shore up the Italian invasion of the continent. Together, the Axis troops fought a long, costly battle against the British, whose forces were strengthened by the entry of the United States into the war in late-1941. The U.S. quickly deployed forces and weaponry to North Africa, pushing the German and Italian military into a series of crippling defeats that resulted in the surrender of the Axis powers on the African continent in the embattled city of Tunisia.

With the defeat of the Axis in North Africa in May 1943, the Allies could turn their attention to mainland Italy and the march north toward Germany. But as other invading forces had done for thousands of years, an approach to the Italian mainland from the south meant pass-

ing through Sicily. By now, the Allies had established very effective battle strategies for their partnership and made swift use of them in their plan to attack the island.

But even with superior forces, the Allied conquest of Sicily was supported by a carefully choreographed deceit conceived by the Allies before they disembarked from North Africa. Late in that campaign, a German detachment found the body of a British pilot in the Mediterranean. In the pilot's possession was a cache of classified documents that detailed the Allied plans to invade Sardinia and Corsica. The secret materials were run up the German chain of command all the way to Adolph Hitler, who ordered German troops to reinforce those islands in preparation to repel the Allies.

As it turned out, the pilot was actually a recent suicide and the Allies had used his body as a decoy, outfitting it with fake documents in an elaborate ruse to lure German forces away from the Allies' actual target – the southern shores of Sicily. The Germans bought into the subterfuge, sent their forces to Sardinia and Corsica, and left the Allies' true objective too lightly defended. The defeat of the Axis forces in Sicily took just over a month. The German and Italian troops were driven from the island.

As North Africa and then Sicily fell to the Allies, the political and military infrastructure of Italy and its ruling Fascist party crumbled. In July 1943, Mussolini was removed from office and arrested. His successor, Pietro Badoglio immediately began secret negotiations with the Allies to join them and sever Italy's ties with Germany.

Meanwhile, American and British forces were driving the remaining Axis troops in Sicily into the far northeastern corner of the island. Unfortunately, the German and Italian soldiers managed to retreat from Messina and go to the mainland, thus avoiding capture. These Axis forces reached southern Italy, occupying the region, and posing another challenge for the Allied forces expecting to enter Italy from the south and march toward Rome.

The surviving Axis troops flooding into southern Italy, presenting a threat to the people there, including the people in the villages of Matera and Altamura.

Chapter 10

On the Train to Toritto

Carlo rode *seconda classe* on a train that left Roma Termini and headed south toward what Italians call the *Mezzogiorno*.

These regions below Rome and Naples are less industrialized, more rural and more sparsely populated. Its cities and villages are ancient, far less modern than those in the north. The *Mezzogiorno's* largely agricultural economy and greater poverty have made southern Italians disparaged as uncultured by the more educated and moneyed classes of the north. This prejudice has persisted for hundreds of years, becoming even more marked after the unification of Italy in the 1860s, a political realignment that rested more power in the urban centers of the north.

Carlo was of southern Italian descent and while he admired Rome and Florence, he was still drawn to the regions where his family originated and to the customs and traditions of a people with deep roots in the past. Riding second class on a train was not a conscious decision, but reflected his embrace of the way of life of those from the *Mezzogiorno*.

As the train rumbled along the tracks south of Rome, Carlo left industrialized centers behind and watched as the landscape turn into a palette of dusky olive and faded taupe. The bright blue sky never lost its crystalline brilliance, but it now hovered over a terrain that seemed drought-ridden and abandoned.

From the window on the train, Carlo gazed out at pastures that seemed to yearn for rain, shepherds tending small herds of gangly sheep, and rivulets of streams that ambled across the flat terrain. As he watched an old farmer in a sweat-stained blue cap drive an old tractor across the rutted farm, a wan smile crept across Carlo's face. He took no pleasure in the scene, just an abject recognition of life in the south and how the tireless efforts of its inhabitants served to provide sufficient sustenance to carry on.

The train made occasional stops in small villages along the route, the station and modest buildings nearby softening the impression of a land lost in time. He bought lunch, a *panino* stuffed with fresh figs, ripe tomatoes, and succulent cheese, and Carlo had to admit that – even in this apparently desolate landscape – Italians still managed to produce mouth-watering food.

As the train lurched once more into motion, he sipped his wine and noted the passing signposts of southern Italy. First Pescara going east, then Foggia on the way south, then Cerignola, Barletta, Molfetta and smaller towns that didn't even warrant a stop. When the train finally pulled into Bari's Centrale station, Carlo was immersed in his memories of Apulia, the region his parents and forebears had grown up in, where some distant cousins still lived and who had hosted him on an earlier trip to Italy.

He collected his bags and disembarked from the train, heading down the *binario*, or platform, toward the rental car company he knew was outside the station. There he rented a Fiat 500, big enough for him but, like most Italian cars, small – and easy to maneuver in cities designed before the invention of automobiles.

Altamura was about a one-hour drive from Bari. Carlo had been in this region before, notably to visit Toritto, his mother's hometown, but he had never driven there before, so navigating the roads became as much a challenge as navigating the pack of caffeine-fueled Italian drivers in the lanes beside him.

Carlo entered Altamura from the Via Bari on the northeastern part of town just as the sun was setting. Instructions mailed to him by the

Filomena family indicated that they lived on Via Cassano delle Murge, south of his present location, but inside the city's border, so he didn't expect it to take long to find their home. Of course, the GPS he relied on in St. Louis wouldn't work in southern Italy, so he was forced to use a more traditional method unfamiliar to a person his age: He stopped to ask for directions.

Carlo rolled down the window of the rental car and pulled alongside a middle-aged man with broad-shoulders and a sun-burned visage.

"*Mi scusi, signore,*" he began, hoping his Italian hadn't languished too long and would soon reappear on his tongue, "*Puo dirmi dov'é la Via Cassano delle Murge?*"

"*Sì,*" the man replied, "*è facile da qui,*" – "it's easy from here."

The man lifted his right arm and, pointing with this index finger which he wagged up and down to make the points in his narrative, he indicated to Carlo that he should drive farther into the city, turn left at Via Santeramo, then left again on Via Cassano. He repeated the directions a second time while Carlo mimicked his words and gestures, nodding his head in understanding.

Carlo had learned most of his Italian dialect at home, featuring the clipped sounds of colloquial *Pugliese*. Fortunately, his knowledge of the dialect – far different from the Florentine Italian taught in the classrooms – would be enough to carry him through his stay in the *Mezzogiorno*.

"*Sì, signore,*" Carlo replied. "*Mille grazie.*"

Chapter 11

Through the Country

As the Italian and German forces headed north, Bernhard's detachment marched down country roads south of Rome, passing small towns, ancient villages, and farms where pastures and vegetable plots lined the roadway. The colonel paid little attention to the pastoral scenery; he was a man of the city and impatient to traverse the open land and settle into one of the more populated centers between Rome and Naples.

They reached Frosinone by nightfall. One of Italy's oldest cities, it had a vibrant economy, complete with local food shops, cafés, restaurants, and a Catholic church. The Nazi troops weren't interested in the church, but they helped themselves to the pleasures of the town. Six of the men sat at a table outside Vittorio's Trattoria, ordering great platters of food and multiple carafes of the local wine. When the bill arrived, they played their familiar game: They examined the bill carefully, rummaged around in their pockets for money, then started fighting among themselves. Their pushing, shoving and feigned anger were enough for the proprietor to eject them from the premises. But before walking away from the table, one man grabbed the half-filled carafe of wine from the table and together the faux-enemies walked away singing songs about the Fatherland.

The southern Italians were often enduring small harvests and times of drought, so food was not abundant even in the best of times. During the years of this war, it was even scarcer, and mothers fought diligently every day to make sure they had enough for their families to survive. The Germans were not only feasting on food that was already in short supply, but their refusal to pay for the meals – true to the example provided by their commanding officer – made an even more indelible impression in the minds of the Italians around them.

Two of the soldiers were observing all this from the bar next door. They laughed at the ruse, all too familiar with it, but kept their attention on the comely waitress who was ordered to serve them by her gray-haired father who was tending to the drinks. One man leered shamelessly at the young lady's bottom while the other allowed himself a pat on the same. When the pat turned into a lingering rub, the owner rushed out to protect his daughter. The two men laughed and pushed him back behind the bar. They, too, left the establishment without paying their bill.

In the morning, Bernhard assembled his men and they drove south out of Frosinone, reaching Cassino in time for the evening meal. The colonel kept to himself, occasionally conferring with Hilgendorf, but he had spied a raven-haired beauty in the piazza and preferred her company to the young lieutenant's. While the Nazi soldiers commandeered the bars, stalked young women through the streets, and acted out their ruse to get free meals, Bernhard settled into his role as visiting royalty. When he discovered where the young woman was heading – Osteria Emanuele – he followed her there and planned to satisfy his hunger with whatever was on the menu, so that he could satisfy his other hunger by getting close to her.

Another day and another town. The German soldiers reached Campobasso and were surprised by the signs of Judaism they found there. Some were on a personal level, the curled locks of hair worn by the men; the modest dress of the women. Some signs were more evident, like the yellow Star of David insignias posted by the occupying German forces on all Jewish business establishments. There had long been a Jewish settlement within the city and segments of the population showed clear evidence of the survival of their culture and religious traditions. While Bernhard dined alone at a sidewalk restaurant, his men brought a man to him. Holding the frightened man by the elbow, one of the soldiers described the situation to his commander.

"He was found lurking around our convoy, sir. Probably planning to steal something."

"No," the man said tremulously. His skull cap left little doubt about his religious affiliation. "I wasn't going to steal anything. I had never seen German cars; I'm a mechanic and was only interested in them."

"Sounds to me like he was planning to steal one," observed the soldier.

"No," pleaded the little Jewish man. "No stealing. No stealing."

Bernhard showed his displeasure at being interrupted during this meal, and so with a wave of his hand, he sent the men away. But, before departing the table, the soldier delivered a violent punch to the man's midsection. The victim doubled over just as his assailant came back with a swift uppercut with his closed fist. The Jew's head rocketed backward, blood spurting from his lips that were split by the impact. As he tried to regain his balance, the victim caught the cold steel of the soldier's handgun across his cheek, breaking his jaw and dropping the poor man to his knees.

Now bored, the soldier simply sneered at the man in the dust, while his companions laughed at the bloodied and broken Jewish mechanic.

Chapter 12

Advancing Into the Invasion, Basilicata, August 1943

Anselm Bernhard sat calmly in the back seat of the German Volkswagen Kübelwagen, a four-seater designed by Ferdinand Porsche and, ironically, built by a U.S. firm in Berlin. The common vehicle for Nazi officers, his was driven by his junior officer, Hilgendorf.

Bernhard couldn't be bothered with reading dispatches from Berlin. He spent the hours riding south past Naples and through the southern towns, peering at the passing landscape. He snorted once, telling Hilgendorf that the southern Italians must be beasts of the earth because their land was barren. He wondered how anyone with promise could live here, then satisfied himself by concluding that the primitive people of the south had no promise, so their environment was fitting.

"Where are we going?" asked the lieutenant.

"South. To Matera," came the answer. Bernhard was searching for more plunder and had heard rumors of a great stash of art that was somewhere in Matera. He didn't feel the need to explain this to Hilgendorf, but the junior officer already knew of his superior's motivation.

Hilgendorf had reason to disagree with his commanding officer in recent days. The news from the south wasn't good and even without benefit of classified dispatches, he and the other dozen men in Bernhard's de-

tachment knew that the Allies had conquered Sicily and were advancing toward the toe of Italy's boot.

His German troops had been pillaging Italian towns and confiscating an assortment of personal items, but they were not happy to be moving south when they could see German divisions moving north to escape the Allied invasion.

"What is in Matera?" asked Hilgendorf. He knew the answer but decided to make the colonel talk about it, so he could discuss the dangers of such a vector.

Bernhard didn't answer. Instead he pulled his notebook from the jacket pocket. Hilgendorf observed over his shoulder that the colonel thumbed past the early entries in the book and stopped at a point several pages from the end. The lieutenant had never looked at the journal; Bernhard would not have allowed it, but Hilgendorf assumed that these last pages held some information of particular importance to the mission.

Bernhard was focused on reading the entries and occasionally made notes on the pages with a pen he kept in the same pocket. Pointing the instrument to a specific entry, he mouthed the words "im erdreich" and then "versteckt," meaning "in the ground," and "hidden." Hilgendorf could sense his concentration but could not turn around to read Bernhard's lips.

The colonel continued to focus on his notes, turning the page, then turning it back again. Without conscious thought, he said, "wie der Sassi." Realizing that he had uttered the words out loud, Bernhard immediately closed the journal and shoved it back into his pocket.

Hilgendorf knew the phrase meant "like the Sassi," but didn't know what Sassi meant.

They drove for another hour in silence then stopped the car and the ones following it under a tree. The shade from this isolated arbor was a relief from the constant heat and sunshine, and the German soldiers lounged for a bit and took longs sips from their canteens of lukewarm water.

Two of the soldiers were talking in hushed tones when Bernhard approached and ordered them to reveal what they were discussing.

"Sir, the Allies are advancing from the south, and our German regiments are retreating to the north," one volunteered. At this, he paused, but then resumed his unplanned speech.

"Why are we going south into the teeth of the American invasion?"

Bernhard didn't feel any obligation to answer the question, but he also knew that dangers were more real here than up in Venice, and he wanted to keep his troops loyal to his cause, selfish though it was.

"There is a great collection in the south, in a dusty little town called Matera. We've been sent there by the Führer to secure the treasure before the Allies destroy it."

Hilgendorf saw several inconsistencies in his colonel's statement. He had no reason to think the Allies would destroy what they were searching for, and he knew that they were not ordered to carry out this mission by the Führer. He also knew the other soldiers suspected as much.

"Will we be able to do this and yet escape before the Americans can take us prisoner?" one of the soldiers asked.

Normally, Bernhard was too controlled to respond to doubts about him or the Third Reich – even though he privately doubted the Nazi establishment himself. But he was also firmly convinced that he had to get to Matera to find the collection and he would not countenance any hesitation from his troops in supporting his mission. In a split second, Bernhard swung the leather glove in his right hand across the face of the man standing in front of him, turning the man's cheek bright red.

The colonel then turned on his heel and marched toward the Kübel-wagen.

Chapter 13

Revenge in Venice, August 1943

The grave was so new that the dirt piled up on the newly interred coffin still bulged at bit at the surface. The surrounding grass would soon spread and overtake this mound, just as the earth itself would settle upon the remains of the departed soul beneath it.

Marisa knelt down at the new head stone that she had arranged to be placed there, a simple flat stone etched with the name of her sister, Alessia, who had killed herself just a few months before. She made the sign of the cross, kissed the rosary beads in her right hand, and stared at the name on the stone.

Her face was blank, her eyes dry, but Marisa's heart burned with a passion for revenge. It bothered her during her everyday routine but troubled her most when she had time to visit Alessia's grave.

"Bastardo," she spit out, "BASTARDO!" she shouted in the empty cemetery at Isola di San Michele.

"You will burn in hell," she continued in a rant, "and I will send you there myself."

Chapter 14

Catching the Devil,
September 1, 1943

Marisa's hands gripped the wheel of the old truck determinedly, intent on narrowing the gap between her and Anselm Bernhard's convoy. She had left Venice several days before and caught up with the colonel's detachment in Rome, but she kept a careful distance until her plan was fully hatched.

On this day, she was only a few miles behind Bernhard as she plotted her revenge. Attacking the Nazi officer broadside would be pointless; his troops would defend him and she would be outnumbered. If she got close enough to poison him, she would, but she wasn't familiar with the science behind such murder scenarios and she couldn't risk failing at her one opportunity.

Marisa had seen Bernhard in the company of his men the day before on the road. She watched him from the approach to the villa near Rome and was able to get quite close by taking advantage of the wine they had imbibed during their bacchanal.

She even allowed herself to slip into the villa, posing as one of the several Roman women conscripted to serve at the evening's dinner. Marisa moved among the drunken men and slid past the group to see the colonel's own quarters. They were all still on the terrazzo and so her snooping around escaped their attention.

Bernhard was a neat and organized man, she concluded. The bedroom was very orderly, the topmost comforter in place as if a maid had arranged them, and his uniform jacket was hung on the wooden rack by the window next to a pair of highly polished boots. Soft electric light streamed from the single lamp that he had next to the bed, and a finely stitched robe was draped elegantly at the foot of the bed.

A sound behind her brought Marisa's attention back to the present danger. She slipped behind a dressing curtain, but then relaxed, realizing that the laughter had passed by the door on the way down the hall.

"This is not the time to be discovered," she thought, "although I would like to stare the bastard in the eye as he draws his last painful breath." A smile crept across her face as she imagined the Nazi's last day on earth, but she had to bring her attention back to her plan to smooth out the details.

As her truck approached a way station along the road, Marisa could see the five vehicles that were part of Bernhard's convoy. She parked a short distance from the only man left to guard them, a long rifle slung over his shoulder. The soldier was smoking a cigarette and drawing sips from a canteen as Marisa walked resolutely by him. His stare made her nervous even though she was used to the men's attentions. She ignored him as she strode past and pushed the door open to the inn and entered the coolness within.

Enough light came through open windows and Marisa's eyes were not initially blinded. She turned her head, scanning one end of the dining room to the other, careful not to linger on the group of German soldiers loudly enjoying their meal at tables in the center of the room.

Marisa noticed that the old man who served them wore a faint, weak smile as he tried to distract the Germans from leering at his young daughter. She was barely sixteen but Bernhard's behavior towards women had apparently infected his troops, leaving them to assume the right to take whatever they wanted.

After a moment, the old man approached and asked Marisa if she wanted a table.

"Sì, lì," *she said, "over there." With her right hand, Marisa indicated the table right next to the Germans. The old man screwed up his wrinkled forehead, and asked if she was sure she wanted to sit so close to the men.*

"Sì, lì," *she said again. The man shrugged, offered a sheepish grin, and directed Marisa to the table she was pointing at.*

She settled into the chair that faced Bernhard and, when he looked over at her, smiled. It was a simple gesture, but she minimized the smile enough to suggest a mixture of interest and caution. It was a coquettish move that a vain man like Bernhard couldn't resist, and his next action proved her to be correct.

The colonel lifted his napkin from his lap and gently stroked the linen across his lips, never letting his eyes leave Marisa. She had looked away, but she knew that he had not.

Rising slowly, Bernhard walked around his own table and towards her. He thrust his shoulders back and snapped his heels together.

"Che piacere," *he said in Italian. "I am pleased to meet someone so beautiful on this lonely road."*

Marisa smiled, but didn't try to stop Bernhard from pulling out a chair and sitting at her table.

"Come ti chiami?" *he asked, "What is your name?" Marisa noted that he used the familiar form for 'you,' a choice that would be considered inappropriate among polite Italians but which this man – even with his command of the language – used to establish immediate intimacy.*

"Marisa," *was her one-word rely. She knew where the conversation was going but she wasn't going to help him along. The role of the coquette required restraint and, until the time was right, resistance.*

"I am Colonel Anselm Bernhard, at your service," *he stated with the formality that could hardly be avoided by a man trained as a German officer.*

He carried on a light conversation with Marisa, although her contributions were few and carefully terse. Bernhard fell for her ploy, unable to resist her charms, and he invited her to join his convoy on the journey to the south.

"But no, sir, I could not attach myself to a military convoy. It would most certainly be wrong and inappropriate for an Italian woman to act in that way."

Bernhard parsed her words, noticing that she specifically stressed propriety for Italian women, as if suggesting that others – Germans? – would have looser morals. But he waved the thought away.

He was considering how to convince her to join him, when Marisa offered a solution.

"Where are you going, my dear Colonel?"

The question was a simple one, but Bernhard couldn't suppress his excitement at being called "dear."

"To Matera. No, actually, to Altamura," he said. Shrugging to his left he added, "We have important business in Matera, but I'm actually staying in Altamura."

"You are staying in Altamura? Where are your men staying?"

"They will be there, somewhere, but..." he began, and leaned forward toward Marisa to say softly, "but who cares where they are. Right?"

Marisa timed her smile for just the right moment. She knew Bernhard was enticed by her lure. So she promised to drive her truck to Altamura.

"I will see you there, non é vero?" she said, fetchingly. It was more a statement than a question.

Sporting a lascivious smile that nearly cleaved his face in two, the colonel returned to his troops and ordered them to rise and resume the trip. At the door, he turned toward Marisa, saluted her and left followed by his men.

Chapter 15

Hidden

Martin Bernhard pulled his car out of the garage at their home in the outskirts of Berlin. His wife was leaving for work at the same time, so he dropped her off at the bus stop, blew her a kiss and reminded her that he would be back from Italy in about a week.

As he swung the car away from the curb, Martin felt pangs of guilt for leaving her again but took solace in knowing that his wife was now fully aware of his activities. He worried that Margrit would be unable to purge notions of his grandfather's activities and think less of the Bernhard family.

Martin and Margrit were members in good standing of the new Germany. They were repelled by the policies of the Third Reich and its massacre of European Jews. And they firmly believed that such a government was not possible in their country today. Hitler and his soulless hatchetmen had put a permanent stain on German history, but Martin was certain that he and his countrymen were born of different stock. He also believed that the guilt that weighed on their collective shoulders would be a constant reminder of the evil that can spread if good people are not vigilant.

Guilt also impelled him to find and return the art stolen from the Italians. By his dedication to the project, the young art collector would show the world that new Germans like himself were not like their ancestors, and that the world could trust them again.

Martin's crusade had successfully returned dozens of paintings and sculptures to their rightful owners. Some he had discovered in Germany were returned thanks to Martin.

Some of the works he found in Italian cities and remote towns, all clearly identified and logged in his grandfather's journal as "confiscated." The journal referred to the works themselves, but unfortunately not the places they ended up in. For that, Martin had to employ greater investigative techniques, starting with references in the journal to women Anselm might have given stolen booty to and the towns these women lived in. Frequently, he had to question locals about artworks in the town, and he made hundreds of fruitless visits to abbeys, churches, bars, markets, and restaurants searching for any piece on Anselm's list.

Then his mind wandered back to his last trip to Italy – years ago, when he had tracked down a painting by a minor 19th century artist, Roberto Melini. He had recognized the stylized brush strokes immediately. This particular work focused on the cityscapes that Melini preferred, another clue that convinced Martin that he had correctly identified the artist.

The painting was one of those listed in his grandfather's journal, along with a note that the Melini had hung in the *Museo Civico Filangieri* in Naples until Anselm had "liberated" it. Martin found it hanging behind the counter in a dimly lit, hole-in-wall bar in a tiny, forgotten town in central Italy. In war, secondary artworks such as this one could become lost, so even the bar owner would not be able to retrace how the little Melini had come into his possession.

Martin contemplated his options, including bargaining with the bar owner for possession of this rare piece, but knew that this might make the man even more possessive of it. Martin then considered acting like a simple customer, enamored of the painting, and try to offer just enough money to buy it from the unsuspecting owner. In the end, Martin simply told the proprietor that the painting had once hung in the museum in Naples, alluding to Nazi thefts without acknowledging his own family's involvement in the affair.

Sensing the bartender's disbelief, Martin retreated to the box of books that he kept in the boot of his car, withdrew one book well-worn from study, and returned to the establishment. He slapped it on the bar and thumbed to a page, then pointed with his right hand to a photograph of the Melini in a chapter describing art lost during the war.

At this point, Martin spun into his usual strategy. He didn't want to have to buy the painting back, only to give it to the museum, but he could try to convince the bar owner that he was in possession of art stolen by the Nazis. After haggling for hours, and together drinking two full bottles of wine, Martin was able to shame the man into giving up the painting.

Martin's memory of the event brought a smile to his lips, which soon turned into a frown. Instead of driving to Naples to return the painting, he arrived home in Germany with it still in the trunk of his car.

When Margrit asked where he had gotten the piece of art – of a type that she wouldn't recognize – Martin shrugged his shoulders and simply said that he found it, liked it, and bought it.

As his thoughts drifted back to the driving at hand, Martin scouted the surroundings for a place to stop and eat a meal. He pulled off the highway, filled the car's gas tank, then settled in for a cup of coffee and a light lunch.

While he chewed his sandwich and sipped the coffee, he flipped through the worn pages of his grandfather's journal. Nearly the entire first half was filled with dated entries describing the art and the women Anselm had admired. Only infrequent entries described the military objectives of the war, and fewer still about the Third Reich's plan for the future world domination. Anselm Bernhard committed the pages of his journal to his own conquests.

There was the marble statue of Venus and three Renaissance-era oil paintings from the museum in Milan; an exquisite sculpture of a winged creature from Greek lore "liberated" from Verona; and oils and a number of sculptures that once graced the walls of private homes in Venice that formed part of Anselm's private collection.

Sandwiched among these entries were graphic descriptions of the women he had slept with. Some of the descriptions were so lurid that Martin became uncomfortable learning the intimate details of his grandfather's relations with these women, details that included what the old man liked to do, and why.

Nearly every description of these sexual encounters included the names of the women. Anselm seemed to take pleasure in revealing their identities as if inscribing them in his book made the conquest more complete.

As Martin finished his meal, he flipped to the back of the journal.

Curiously, those pages held no descriptions of great art or voluptuous women. The notes in the back of the journal were cryptic references to a treasure with phrases like "under the ground," "in the earth," and "hidden from view" that puzzled him. His grandfather seemed to be writing down everything he came across that related to that one undiscovered trove, even snippets of conversation as if he had been trying to piece together enough information to solve a mystery.

Martin studied the notes again. It was clear that whatever Anselm was searching for when he took his detachment of German soldiers south was a great cache of art or wealth, hidden somewhere – probably under the ground – in southern Italy. The notes included occasional references to small towns in the region, with Matera mentioned most often. The journal revealed that his grandfather had settled in Altamura, a town near Matera, but had focused his search on Matera itself.

Then, on the last page, a familiar passage suddenly become clearer to Martin. It referred to the *Sassi* as caves where scores of Italians lived. From the personality that came to life in the pages of the journal, Martin imagined Anselm's self-important grunt when he read the words, "damn animals."

The young art collector had seen the word *Sassi* before and researched it for any assistance in his quest. The *Sassi* were indeed caves carved into the hillside of the mountain called the Murge, neighboring both Altamura and Matera. The caves had been there for thousands of years and, over the centuries, had become more complex and artistic, and where entire families could live in comfort. Some of the people of the *Sassi* even carved out elaborate chapels in the hillside, and leveled roads above one row of caves as byways for the caves cut on the level above.

Italians had lived in these caves for many generations and still occupied them during World War II. The religious structures in the *Sassi*, known as *sante grotte* or "holy caves," completed the impression of a civilization surviving on the edge of the Murge with everything that ancient and modern Italians would want.

Martin thought of the caves merely as odd artifacts of a primitive society, although he couldn't dismiss the ingenuity that had gone into creating them. Then he returned to the German words he had seen scrawled in his grandfather's journal.

"*Verstect*" – hidden.

"*Im erdreich*" – in the ground.

"*Wie der Sassi*" – like the *Sassi*.

One last word jumped out at him that morning.

"*Kirche*" – church.

"Did grandfather suspect that the artworks were hidden in a church?" he murmured to himself. "Under the ground?

"No, not 'under the ground'... In the ground, like the *Sassi*."

Martin knew there was a church in the caves of the *Sassi*. Could it be that his grandfather had discovered, or at least suspected, that the fortune he was seeking was hidden in the church of the *Sassi*?

Chapter 16

Retracing the Steps

After hours on the road, Martin headed south through Italy, still lost in thought about his grandfather's journal. Even by the quickest route, the journey took an entire day, south on the A9 then A14 along Italy's eastern coast. He had spent most of his trips to Italy searching the cities along the route taken by Anselm in 1943. This trip drove him farther south than he had ever been, but was consistent with the course that the colonel had taken so many years before toward Altamura.

Traffic along the Adriatic coastal highway was not the problem, but the frequent construction sites were, and these slowed Martin's trip to Altamura. The itinerary took him past towns that he would have liked to explore, like the Republic of San Marino, an independent sovereign nation within Italy. He assumed that gaining entry to it would slow him down and he still had many miles to cover before arriving in the towns in southern Italy where he would resume his quest.

At Ancona, Martin left the highway to have a quick dinner. His upbringing ensured his commitment to German cuisine, but he nevertheless enjoyed the supper he was served at *La Taverna Adriatica*. Drawing from the nearby Adriatic Sea, this highway *trattoria* offered *frutti di mare*, or fried catch of the day including *arrosto segreto,* stuffed roasted sardines. The main course was *crocette in porchetta*, sea snails roasted with fennel, rosemary, garlic, and olive oil – as one would roast a pig – *in porchetta*. All accompanied by freshly baked crusty bread infused with olives and rosemary. Martin passed up the proffered red wine so he could stay awake for the remaining five hours on the road, but he marveled at the display of food on his plate.

"How can a people thought to be so poor eat so well?" he thought. "Even at a simple highway restaurant!"

He finished the *crocette,* mopping the juices with the bread from the basket on the table, wiped his mouth, checked his shirt for accidental drippings and, seeing none, stood up from the table. The small white piece of paper next to his plate described the meal, which he took to the cashier's desk at the door. A middle-aged woman with smiling eyes under wisps of gray hair looked up from reading *La Stampa* and took his money, a meager twelve euros for the repast.

"*Grazie. Arrivederla,*" she said, sending Martin off into the cool air of the evening and back to his car for the drive south.

"*Arrivederci,*" he replied. Martin's mastery of Italian had improved over the many trips to the country, but he was not fluent and so he entered into only brief exchanges with the people there. Like many Europeans, he easily spoke three languages, German, English, and Spanish, and had developed a passing familiarity with Italian.

As the sun set and the temperature dropped, Martin drove south along the highway through towns and hamlets: San Benedetto, Montesilvano, and Pescara. Just south of Termoli, the highway veered away from the sea and turned inland. He passed San Severo, Foggia, and Cerignola, where he left the A14 and took a minor road to Altamura.

He spent some time finding the Hotel San Nicola, an 18th century hotel that had been modernized, and parked his car. Located at Via Luca de Samuele Cagnazzi 29, this hotel had a restaurant – which in Italy meant they also served wine and cocktails in the lobby – making Martin glad that he had chosen this establishment. A quickly downed glass of chilled white wine followed by a more calmly sipped red wine helped to clear the road dust from his throat and, once in his room, lull him into a deep sleep.

The morning sun shone through the thin curtains and woke Martin up earlier than he had wanted. Through squinting eyes, he looked at the room, turned over, and considered going back to sleep. But the journal was on the nightstand and spoke to him.

"*Im erdreich...wie der* Sassi."

Before retiring the night before, Martin had done a little more research on the *Sassi* on his mobile phone. It referred to the caves but the term was sometimes also used to refer to the people who inhabited them. The grottoes were carved into the hillside and, therefore, could be considered "in the ground...like the *Sassi*" and Martin understood his grandfather's notes to suggest that the riches he sought were probably in those caves.

Once distracted by so many thoughts Martin couldn't return to sleep so he rose grudgingly from the bed and showered, preparing for a new day.

Once down in the hotel lobby, Martin waited while a pair of elderly American ladies questioned the desk clerk.

"We heard that the true Saint Nicholas is from this area. Is that right?" one asked.

The clerk was familiar with the story and knew that the people of Puglia and Basilicata claimed the saint of Christmas lore as their own. He also knew that San Nicola was a 4th century Greek bishop who had died in Greece but whose bones had been brought to Bari and interred there. The relic brought Christian pilgrims and launched the centuries-long legend of the saint as the Santa Claus of gift-giving.

The hotel clerk knew the facts but, more importantly, also knew the value of San Nicola and the tourist dollars that the legend brought to Bari and the region of Puglia, which at times shared its notoriety with bordering Basilicata region. The hotel was in fact named after the saint and these money-wielding Americans should be reassured that they were patronizing the region where the true Santa Claus once lived. "Well," the clerk thought silently, "at least he is buried here."

"*Sì*, ladies," he said with confidence. "Santa Claus is from here." One of the women asked where was he buried, but her companion quickly jumped in.

"You can't bury Santa Claus, Karen."

"Well, it's not like he was Jesus Christ!" the other one replied. They wandered off deep in debate about where Santa Claus could be found, having forgotten that the original question was put to the clerk at the desk.

When it was his turn, Martin approached the desk and smiled at the clerk.

"I understand that San Nicola's bones are actually in Venice," Martin said.

The clerk frowned and, with a shrug of the shoulders, admitted that this was one of the theories thrown around by those who fought over the saint's celebrity.

"*Beh,*" he muttered. "Many cities claim the holy saint as their own, but the bones in Venice are not his."

Martin didn't want to dispute this or enter into a debate with the man. He knew from his research – and his grandfather's journal – that the bones in Venice are believed to represent some of San Nicola's remains, although he also knew that most of the holy man's bones were interred here in this region, as the proud locals claimed.

"I am a German museum collector and I have been sent to find lost Italian art, materials that may have been removed during the war."

The clerk's sideways glance put Martin on alert, so he tried to clarify.

"My hope is that some of the artwork that was removed during the Second World War could be found, and perhaps returned to the churches and homes that had lost them."

The people in Altamura and the greater region of Basilicata knew all too well about the Italian wealth that was taken by the Germans. "Removed during the war" was a phrase that hardly described the crimes committed by the Nazis. To the hotel clerk, his German visitor was a modern-day version of the Nazi thieves who plundered his country seventy years ago.

The clerk looked down at the register, laid his index finger upon a certain entry, then turned toward Martin.

"You are in room 102, *sì*?"

"Yes."

"Signor Bernhard, *giusto?*"

"Yes."

The clerk studied Martin's face for several seconds, then resumed with tightened lips.

"Are you any relation to the German general, Anselm Bernhard?"

"Actually, he was a colonel," Martin said, quickly realizing his mistake. By correcting the facts about his grandfather's identity, he had fallen into the clerk's trap, and inadvertently revealed his connection to Bernhard.

"*Colonel* Bernhard," the clerk responded slowly, emphasizing the man's rank, "is well known in Altamura. And you say you are an art collector?"

"Yes, but you see, I am not my grandfather." Martin could already tell that backpedaling at this point in the conversation was a strategic error. Looking down at his hands gripping the railing of the desk, he continued.

"Like many of the Nazis at the time, my grandfather committed crimes against the Italian people. I cannot justify his actions, and my apologies would no doubt seem inadequate. I have spent many months traveling throughout Italy searching for and returning the artworks my grandfather stole. I am here, in Altamura, to continue that mission."

He looked at the clerk, who seemed unmoved by this quasi-confession.

"It is my hope that I can restore most, if not all, the stolen works to their rightful owners. Anselm Bernhard will burn in hell, but I hope to re-establish the good name of Germany by undoing some of his sins."

Martin had planned to ask the clerk for directions to the *Sassi*, but this conversation left him feeling quite unnerved, and he decided that pursuing the plan would be pointless. So he retired to the breakfast room where he ate his *prima colazione* alone.

Chapter 17

Benvenuto

When he arrived in Altamura the night before, Carlo had wandered a bit searching for the Filomena household then came upon it suddenly. It was just turning to dusk when he arrived, and the lights in the house were ablaze in anticipation of his arrival.

The family friend in St. Louis had written to Elena and Cristiano Filomena twice already, priming them for Carlo's expected visit. So when he stepped through the doorway, Carlo didn't feel like he was confronting strangers. Handshakes quickly turned into hugs, and rapid-fire questions in colloquial Italian had Carlo's head spinning. Their daughter, Giovanna, emerged from another room soon enough to rescue the guest from this onslaught of questions.

The broad table in the middle of the main room quickly filled up with fragrant plates of roasted meat and bowls of grilled vegetables. Pasta soon emerged from the kitchen, and Carlo wondered how something so dependent on timing could be produced just moments after his arrival.

Cristiano proudly set two bottles of wine on the table. They were label-less and looked the same to Carlo, so he wondered why two bottles were served at the same time. Gia anticipated Carlo's confusion and whispered in standard Italian, "Papa knows that one bottle would never be enough for four of us, so he's just saving a trip to the cellar."

At that she grinned and patted Carlo on the arm, as if to reassure him in his entry into true Italian life.

Conversation never dragged that night, and Carlo did his best to keep up, but the dialect didn't always translate easily into his standard Italian. This is where Gia's formal education came in handy. More than a few times, she repeated what her parents were saying in standard Italian instead of dialect, so that Carlo could catch on.

After a long trip, a few hours of driving, and a sumptuous meal, Carlo slept soundly that night. He woke to bright sunshine that streamed in through a window whose drapes had been pulled apart with a dramatic sweep of Zia Filomena's arms.

"*Buon giorno!*" she said cheerfully. Her salt and pepper hair was pinned carelessly back from the sides of her face, revealing chubby cheeks and dazzling dark green eyes. A smile lit up her face when she saw Carlo squint in the light, but she wasn't about to let him sleep any longer.

The villagers called Elena Filomena "*Zia*" out of respect for her and her baking skills, but also as a term of endearment. The roly-poly woman was always in good spirits, always seeming to smell like the fabulous bread she spent most days baking, and always offering a quote from the Bible to remind lesser humans how they were expected to act. She wasn't a book-toting Christian like those "reborn" in America, but she relied on the verses of the Bible to inform and direct her life – and the lives of those under her charge.

Zia's husband, Cristiano, was much in need of her supervision. Years of hard physical labor in the fields had left him with a slightly stooped posture, but his ruddy complexion and ready smile conveyed a man who had a happy life.

Despite the invisible weight that seemed to sit upon his shoulders, he was strong and healthy. His strength belied the nearly 60 years he had lived. He was devoted to his wife and daughter, but Zia knew that Cristiano was also in love with the wine that he made from vines grown on the outskirts of their town. With her oversight, which Cristiano lamely complained of from time to time, Zia expected her husband – and their marriage – to last for many more years.

Gia was their daughter. Her proper name was Giovanna, but everyone took to calling her by the shortened name, except her mother. Zia believed that some degree of formality was a good thing in families and preferred that her daughter go by her given name, not some Americanized shorter version. But Cristiano liked to use the diminutive form of the name for his beloved daughter, and so did Gia's friends.

"Time to get up. The coffee is getting cold," Zia announced as she swept out of the room.

Carlo dressed quickly, stumbled down the hallway to the tiny bathroom on his way to the kitchen downstairs. Since he had arrived about dinner time the night before, he had met the family but had too little time to get to know them. That morning, he hoped to change that.

The coffee wasn't getting cold. In fact Zia hadn't even made the small pot of espresso. Carlo soon found out that "the coffee is getting cold" was a phrase Zia used to remind people to hurry things up a bit. *Prima colazione* in the Filomena house was much like that in other Italian homes, fresh rolls and some fruit, accompanied by cups of bracing espresso or foamy cappuccino. While he consumed this he listened to the banter among mother, father, and daughter, his eyes darting from face to face as he tracked their comments.

There was enough Italian spoken by Carlo's parents and friends in the neighborhood on The Hill in St. Louis that Carlo had developed a familiarity with it. Their Italian was southern, like that spoken in Altamura and in the Filomena household. With dialects so powerful a force in Italy, and the differences in phrasing, vocabulary, and idioms between the regions, Carlo silently thanked his background for teaching him the dialect of the region. But the conversations he was used to on The Hill came at a slower pace, not with the burst of energy he noticed here that made it so hard for Carlo to keep up.

"*É ora*," said Zia. It didn't take long for Carlo to realize this was another of Zia's favorite phrases. "It's time" was the signal for all those around her to get in gear and move on to the business of the day.

Gia had already risen from the table and was cleaning up the dishes when Cristiano stood up and walked out the door.

"He always spends the morning in the vineyard," said Giovanna. "We don't think he's actually working out there, but he likes to spend time with the grapes."

"And the wine," added Zia Filomena with a wink.

A slight smile crept across Carlo's face. He began to recognize some of the gender-specific stereotypes some Italian families back in St. Louis also evinced. The men didn't regard the women as second class – and the women certainly didn't regard their men as the rulers of the family – but there was a fixed distribution of labor honored by tradition that was apparent to Carlo even here.

"*É ora*," Zia said again. "Time that we begin baking the bread."

With that she swung her head to the side, indicating that Carlo should follow her. They stepped out into the sunlight and Zia turned toward an arched stone hemisphere next to the house. It looked like a very small oven, but Carlo knew right away it wasn't.

In fact, the stone enclave was the opposite of an oven. It was on the shaded side of the house so the stone would remain cool. Zia reached inside the opening and withdrew a clay bowl that was mounded on top and covered with a cloth. She called Carlo's attention to the bowl, then drew back a corner of the cloth to reveal a large ball of dough.

The stone structure stored the dough to allow it to begin rising. Kept warm but away from searing heat, the yeast and starch acted together to begin a fermentation process similar to that which turns grape juice into wine. The result was a bulging lump of yeasty dough that, when properly kneaded, rounded, and cuffed, would turn into the crusty bread for which Altamura was justly famous, the *Pane di Altamura*.

Wagging her finger and smiling, Zia Filomena knew what Carlo's first question would be.

"No special yeast or chemicals, like they use in the America," she explained. "Here, in Altamura, the yeast comes from the clay and the building and the ovens we bake our loaves in. It's like a spirit in the air that comes to enrich our bread and feed our families."

Cristiano, coming around a corner, quickly added, "and ferment our grapes and slake our thirst."

Zia Filomena slapped him on the shoulder and both of them shared a laugh, as Carlo stood watching the faithful and happy couple.

Chapter 18

A Morning of Baking Bread

Zia Filomena reached into the little stone cave again and withdrew another bowl covered with a cloth. The aromas of this bread were more obvious to Carlo, as the scent of garlic and rosemary escaped from the dough she held.

Zia handed the bowl to Carlo and told him to follow her.

As they strode down the street, they met women supervising little children at play, some others dusting the window frames and balconies of their houses, and some of the neighborhood mothers who were carrying risen dough for their own bread baking. Like Italian villages through the centuries, in Altamura communal ovens were located around the town where most of the bread baking took place. Ovens in the homes were used for meat, casseroles, and other single family repasts, but communal ovens held special advantages not easily achieved in one's home.

For one, bread baking requires a much hotter oven than one used for cooking, and wood burning ovens provided a crisp finish to the loaves not possible in gas or electric ovens. So the women of Altamura insisted on using the communal ovens as their ancestors had done and maintained this throwback to past traditions with love and attention.

In this neighborhood, the oven sat in the middle of a small square, too small to be considered a piazza yet large enough to host a bread oven with two ports on the side and a large wood-stoked fire burning in the interior. The wood was piled in the middle of the oven, usually early in the morning before the men headed off to the farmland outside the village. It was allowed to burn to a heated brilliance for a few hours. The prolonged combustion heated up the stones of the oven, and would be tended and fed throughout the day.

By mid-morning, the stones of the oven were hot enough to begin baking and the women of the neighboring streets came with the loaves they had prepared after breakfast. The dough balls would be shaped then slashed with a mark – some like an "x"; others just parallel markings – distinctive for each family so the finished products could be reclaimed by the owners after baking. Each woman, in turn, would toss some corn meal on a great wooden paddle fitted with a long handle, and the loaves would be slid into the oven around the perimeter, equally far from the wood fire and the heated stones that shaped the dome of the oven.

Every few minutes, the women would reach into the fiery interior with the paddles, pushing and rotating the loaves, occasionally checking each for doneness, but never interrupting the continuing banter among the gathered bakers. This was a time of socializing for the ladies, and the hour or so spent at the oven was a precious time that none wanted to miss.

Stories were told about the families, the events in Altamura and the region, and – always – the activities of their children. Some of the stories were ribald, as the mothers recounted the dating habits of their children and others. This morning was no exception, and Carlo's presence made for some friendly jesting, since the men of the town were seldom privy to the conversations of these women at the oven.

Zia Filomena grasped her paddle in two hands, shoved it into the oven then poked around the interior. Carlo was watching her movements and studying her method of minding the loaves, while Zia's friends studied him. When Zia was finished tidying up the loaves and their position in the oven, she looked at Carlo to see if he was paying attention, then laughed when she realized that the circle of middle-aged women seemed more interested in the young man than the bread in the oven.

"*Fermatevi*," she said, "stop," although she laughed. "Do you want black bricks for your dinner tonight, or bread?"

Carlo suddenly noticed what was going on around him and blushed. To cover his embarrassment, he quickly switched to questioning Zia Filomena

"Do you time the baking?"

Wagging a finger, Zia replied, "*No, no*, only by touch." She gestured this last phrase with her index finger, poking downward at a make-believe loaf of bread.

Carlo knew this would hardly extract him from the center of attention, but hoped to divert the attention and appear to be concentrating on the baking process. But the blood was slow to subside from his cheeks.

Chapter 19

The Art of the Vine

Cristiano observed the activities from a respectful distance. By this time in the morning, he would usually be in the vineyard but, leaving the house, he suspected that this young guest might need to be rescued from the ovens, so he wandered close to the square and sat at a café table, smoking a Toscano cigar and sipping espresso till the right moment.

"Carlo," he called out, *"vieni qua,"* – "come here."

It sounded vaguely like an order, not an invitation, but Carlo appreciated the opportunity to remove himself from the circle of women. Bread baking was a patient art and he could learn more later.

He sat down at Cristiano's table and smiled at him wanly. The older man knew what was happening, and Carlo knew that he had been given a reprieve.

"Baking bread is a fine art in this village. Altamura is famous throughout Italy, probably the whole world," Cristiano said with exaggerated pride. "And the women of our little town are famous for it." Leaning toward Carlo and pointing his index finger at him, Cristiano added, "And my wife is without question the best of them all," raising that index finger to the sky to make the point.

"But sometimes the women must be left to their own, *non è vero?*" he added.

"*Sì,*" came Carlo's simple reply, "agreed."

"*Sì*," Cristiano repeated. "We are visited by the spirit...," something that Carlo recalled hearing that morning from Zia Filomena.

"Zia talked of that when we were collecting the rising dough for the oven. The spirit is the yeast?"

"*Sì*, the yeast that ferments both the bread and the wine of Altamura. In your country, winemakers use yeast they get out of jars." Cristiano spat out this last word as if it was a crime.

"Well, not so much anymore," came Carlo's retort. He didn't know a lot about commercial winemaking in America, but he had made wine with his father and uncles, and he knew enough that propagated yeast – often lamely called "commercial yeast" – intended for winemaking was being replaced in some cases with natural yeast by some more resourceful winemakers.

Still, Carlo accepted Cristiano's disdain for the propagated yeast without compliant, even while he felt compelled to defend his own country and remind his elderly patron that the best winemakers in America respected the difference and tried to find a compromise between the gap in styles.

"*Sì, sì*," said Cristiano impatiently, "but here there is no dispute. Natural yeast, the spirit in the air, is what makes our wine and bread. We don't have to debate it; it is plain to see."

With that, he tapped Carlo on the shoulder. "*Andiamo*," he said, standing and beckoning Carlo to follow him.

They walked side by side past several streets, back to the Filomena house. When Cristiano ducked inside the doorway to his own home, he again waved his hand at Carlo, instructing him to follow.

They walked past the dining area and kitchen, where Carlo paused to wave at Giovanna at the stove. Cristiano then led Carlo into a back room through a heavy oaken door. It was not a cellar – the room was above ground – but it served as Cristiano's winery. Bulbous oak casks and large demijohns of glass lined the walls. Assorted instruments of winemaking hung from pegs on the walls. Ancient, gnarled, wooden racks held hundreds of bottles of wine, and an old wine press stood guard in a corner of the room.

Cristiano entered the room without intending to impress Carlo because, for him, the trappings of the small Filomena winery were nothing out of the ordinary. All Cristiano wanted was to treat Carlo to one of his bottles of wine.

The old man pulled a bottle from the rack. None had labels, but Cristiano's actions were focused and clear. He knew which bottle he wanted and – Carlo assumed – knew which vintage to secure, before setting the bottle on an aged wooden table in the middle of the room.

Cristiano reached for a corkscrew on a peg above the wine racks and set about driving it into the bottle gripped in his left hand. With a subtle "pop," he pulled the cork as wondrous and fruity aromas filled the air. Cristiano poured two glasses half full and set the bottle down on the table.

"*Salute!*" he said. "To your health."

As Carlo raised his glass he examined the wine's deep ruby color. Simple house wines were not meant to be studied and for Carlo to examine this too closely would be an insult to this host.

Cristiano took a hearty gulp, which Carlo mimicked. The wine was silky smooth, with a fruity mouthfilling flavor, and it went down softly without any aftertaste. Among the elegant wines of the world it would be forgotten, but as a simple, table wine it was wonderful.

"What is it? I mean, what are the grapes you use?"

"Primitivo," Cristiano replied. "I think your winemakers in California call it Zinfandel."

The origins of Zinfandel had been traced to Puglia and DNA tests suggested that it is derived from the Primitivo grape. He accepted the science, but he had to admit that the two wines were very different. The Zinfandel of California was more pronounced and spicy; the Primitivo that he was enjoying at that moment was smoother and had what he could only call more elegance.

Cristiano explained the process he used for winemaking, beginning with the harvest of grapes in the fields outside Altamura and ending with the heavy lifting required during the bottling phase.

"Most of our families don't bottle their wines," he admitted. "They keep the wine in barrels or demijohns. But I like to bottle it and serve just a bit at a time. It keeps the rest of the wine from spoiling too quickly, and" he continued with a wink, "you can send greedy drinkers home after a bottle or two, before they've cleaned out an entire batch."

Chapter 20

La Passeggiata

That evening, after *cena*, or supper, Giovanna took Carlo to the main square of Altamura for the evening *passeggiata*, a ritual event for families to get together in the *piazze* where they walk arm in arm, striking up conversations with friends who were also sharing the evening air.

Zia and Cristiano went along and, just behind them, came Gia and Carlo. She was already comfortable enough with her house guest that she slipped her hand through his arm as they walked, and she pointed to friends, calling out "*ciao*" and "*buona sera*" frequently, and telling Carlo about the people of Altamura.

Gia had the olive complexion, dark eyes, and luxurious tresses common to her heritage as a southern Italian woman. Her eyes smiled along with her lips, and she took great pleasure in telling Carlo about the young couples she pointed out along the edges of the piazza.

"Oh, you would not be able to resist her," she claimed, indicating a voluptuous young woman named Diana who was being courted by no less than three men. "She is the, the... what do you call the most beautiful girl in America?"

"Miss America?" he offered.

"*Sì, sì!*" Gia's description of Diana bore no hint of jealousy. Carlo could see the Gia too was very attractive, and he noticed the attention that she got from the young men they passed.

"Ah, Arabella!" Gia exclaimed. She pulled her hand from Carlo's elbow and threw her arms around the neck of a striking girl who had just entered the square.

"*Come stai?*" she asked, "how are you?"

"*Molto bene, grazie,*" came the answer. "Very well, thanks."

Carlo took advantage of the girls' chat to appraise Arabella. She had light, almost blond hair, and crystalline blue eyes highlighted by the light touch of eyeliner applied above and below. Her cheeks were a soft pinkish red, but not from blush.

Her dress was modest, but a scooping neckline showed off her figure, and the tight sash across her waist emphasized her shapeliness. He picked up on Gia's comments about him – "*Viene dagli degli Stati Uniti*" she said, "he comes from the United States," and noticed Arabella smiling back at him.

"*Carlo, ti presento la mia amica, Arabella,*" said Gia, gently pushing her friend closer to Carlo. Arabella offered her hand to shake, though Carlo was unsure of the appropriate response. A handshake seemed a bit too American, but he really didn't have a firm understanding yet of Italian etiquette. He accepted Arabella's offer though, taking her hand lightly in his.

"Carlo is visiting us to learn more about life among Italians," Gia explained. "He thought he would just watch and observe us, eat our meals and meet our pretty ladies." At this, Carlo blushed. "But mama has him baking bread and papa, well, you know my father, he has Carlo enjoying the fruits of the vine."

"No, well yes," he stammered. "But my main interest is in learning more about Italian life. You see, I'm Italian-American and..." His voice trailed off when the two young ladies in front of him seemed to lose interest.

"Come," Gia said, taking Carlo's right arm. At the same moment, Arabella took hold of his left arm, and Carlo blushed thinking that he was now escorting two beautiful women on *la passeggiata*.

They walked around the piazza while Gia and Arabella talked back and forth in front of Carlo, nodding and gesturing with their free arms.

The conversation was lively, punctuated by occasional giggles or outright laughter, but Carlo was enjoying every second of it.

"Alessandro has been spending a lot of time around Giulia's house," said Gia.

"*Sì*," replied her friend, "and I don't think her papa likes it very much. How about Giada?" she said, pointing to an auburn-haired woman sitting at the cafè.

Gia giggled, then frowned. They both knew Giada, and didn't particularly get along with her, but such were the ways among competitive young people.

"How long will you stay?" Arabella suddenly asked Carlo. The conversation up to that point had been in Italian, which he followed, but Carlo realized that he had not heard Arabella speak in English until she addressed him.

"Um, I don't know. Probably for a couple of weeks."

At that instant, Gia pulled her arm from his, smiled at them, and spun away to talk to another friend standing nearby. Arabella and Carlo were left alone and, to his estimation, this had been planned by his adopted "sister."

"So, *due settimane*?" Arabella said.

"*Sì*, two weeks," he replied as they resumed their walk.

"Okay," Arabella commented, slipping her arm further around Carlo's. "Then I'll tell you all about the people of Altamura."

Chapter 21

La Chiesa dello Spirito Santo

Like most Italian towns, Sunday mornings in Altamura have a different routine from the other days of the week. Dressed in their best clothes, Zia Filomena, Cristiano, Gia, and Carlo walked several streets to the broad stone steps of La Chiesa dello Spirito Santo, the Church of the Holy Spirit. They exchanged greetings as they made their way through the crowd entering the church. Carlo spotted Arabella but, to his disappointment, she avoided his gaze.

The interior of the church was cool and calm, with the stillness broken only by an organ's melodic promenade leading churchgoers to their seats. The Filomena family – plus one – ducked into a pew four rows from the altar.

The Latin mass had been abandoned decades before in favor of services in Italian. But Carlo noticed that here, in Italy, the vernacular was much closer to the Latin version and it reminded him of the rare instances when the mass was said at St. Ambrose church in St. Louis in Italian instead of English.

An elderly man lit the candles. His thinning hair revealed a shiny pate and his broad frame bore simple work clothes neatly pressed for the Sunday service. Carlo saw a serenity in the man's face that seemed to feed on the peaceful ritual taking place at the altar, and the American visitor envied the man's inner calm.

Standing, kneeling, sitting, and singing hymns commanded every-one's participation, even those with obviously deficient vocal talent. Carlo joined in, but tried hard not to embarrass his hosts by torturing notes that he never felt were within his range. After the Eucharist was offered and the final benediction given, the parishioners slowly filed out of the church into the late morning sunshine.

Zia and Cristiano lingered near the door of La Chiesa dello Spirito Santo, talking to friends while Gia and Carlo talked about the coming events of the day. After a few moments more, the priest, Don Adolfo appeared in the doorway. He was wrinkled, gray, and stooped over. Carlo estimated his age to be about 90, but the elderly priest smiled in the sunshine and strongly grasped people's hands as he worked the crowd.

Don Adolfo approached Cristiano and Zia, offered a handshake for the man and salutation for the lady, and was introduced to Carlo.

"He is visiting from America," Giovanna explained, but Carlo interrupted her.

"*Piacere, padre,*" he began, "pleased to meet you, father. I have grown up in an Italian-American family and have great respect for the Italian culture. I want to spend time in your wonderful town to learn more about Italian families and what makes them so special."

"What makes them so special?" Don Adolfo said, with a sly smile of amusement. "What makes them so special is that they stay together, loving each other, and carrying the Lord in their hearts." He said this with conviction, nodding his head to stress the truth of his statement.

"And you are Catholic, yes?" asked Don Adolfo. Carlo nodded, knowing that this was not the time to debate the details of the marginalization of American Catholicism.

"*Va bene,*" replied Don Adolfo, with Zia, Cristiano, and Gia nodding their heads. "Very well. And I hope you will attend Mass regularly while you are here."

Carlo offered his assurances and shook the priest's hand. Don Adolfo's grip had a firmness that Carlo hadn't expected from such an old man. The priest made the sign of the cross on their parting.

Turning away from Don Adolfo, Carlo noticed the elderly man from the candle lighting standing among the pews of the church. He carried himself erect and appeared to possess a physical strength that belied his age, which Carlo estimated to be about seventy. The man was busy arranging the hymnals left behind by the parishioners and turned only momentarily toward the people outside the church.

He nodded to Carlo and gave a slight smile.

"That's Nino," Gia explained, whispering in Carlo ear. "He's very nice but a bit unusual. He's very quiet, some people think he's not right in the head."

"He's fine in the head," Cristiano protested. "Maybe he's not as smart as your friends at the university, but he keeps the church tidy and works hard in maintaining it."

"Nino lives around back, in a little house attached to Don Adolfo's residence," said Zia. "He takes care of La Chiesa dello Spirito Santo and the convent that is part of it."

Gia took her parents' words as a rebuke. "I wasn't trying to speak ill of Nino, but he does seem a bit slow."

Carlo watched the man walk back into the church, carrying stacks of hymn books with him.

Chapter 22

Seeking out the Sassi

After breakfast at Hotel San Nicola, Martin returned to his room to collect some things for his day's activities. He put his camera, guidebook, and Italian-German dictionary into his back pack. He sat on the bed for a moment, thumbing through his grandfather's journal until he reached the back. The phrases his grandfather left and the short narrative paragraphs focused his attention on this town and the *Sassi* that were cut into the nearby hillsides. There was nothing said directly about the Murge, the plateau that dominated the topography of this region, so he consulted the guidebook to get a better understanding of the area.

He carefully placed the old journal in his pocket and left the room, quietly closing the wooden door behind him. He proceeded down the stone steps that led to the lobby and straight out into the daylight. After his earlier encounter with the desk clerk, he didn't expect to get any guidance from the man about the *Sassi*, so Martin knew he would have to ask for help elsewhere.

It was only half past eight so the sun was up but it was not yet hot. Martin decided to find a seat at a nearby café to allow himself more time to consult the journal and his travel guide and, hopefully, find a waiter or other staff willing to tell him more about the *Sassi*.

"*Buon giorno*," said his waiter rather curtly. "What would you like?" he continued in stilted German. Martin realized the waiter could tell he was German by the travel guide on the table.

"*Un espresso, per favore*," Martin said, hoping to get on the waiter's good side. A few moments later the man returned with a small cup and saucer.

"*I* sassi..." Martin began, "*sono vicini?*" – "they are near here?"

The question seemed lame even to Martin, since it was fairly common knowledge that the famous caves were a destination for many tourists. The hillside had been eroded over the millennia by the Gravina River, cutting a ravine upon the face of which the *Sassi* were dug.

"*I sassi?*" the waiter asked.

"*Sì*, the *Sassi*." Switching back to English, Martin pressed on. "I have heard much about them and I would like to learn more, perhaps visit them. Are they off limits?"

"*No, signor, non è vietato l'accesso.*" Access is not forbidden.

"But they are so old," Martin continued. "I just assumed that they would be held as precious ancient buildings."

"*Sì*, they are old, and they are, as you say, *preziosi*, but we have lived in them for many centuries."

"Not now," Martin said with conviction.

"*No, no signore*, not now," the waiter corrected, "but the people of Basilicata and Puglia lived in the *Sassi* until the 1950s."

The guidebook indicated that the United Nations had declared the *Sassi* to be a World Heritage Site, but said nothing about humans living in the caves until so recently.

"That's not possible, is it?" he asked the waiter.

"*Certo, certo*," said the waiter, now warming to Martin. "People of this area, Matera in particular, lived in the caves until after the Second World War. The government forced them out in the 1950s, but we still hear stories about the Sassi and their people."

Martin quickly considered the implications of this. If the waiter was right, and if his grandfather's search led him to the *Sassi* during World

War II, the colonel would have encountered Italian peasants still occupying the caves where he believed the art and jewels to be.

But it also supported Anselm Bernhard's notion that the great cache of art would be in the *Sassi*. "*Im erdreich*" might mean in the ground, but wouldn't it be safer to protect the hidden treasure with sentries who still occupied the caves?

"How can I go there? Do I need a guide?"

The waiter thought about the request, peering at the sky as if looking for the answer.

"No, a guide is not necessary, but my cousin knows the *Sassi* well. He has been there many times, and I'm sure he would like to explain them to you."

"Good. Thank you," said Martin. "How can I meet him?"

Chapter 23

Establishing Trust

Martin waited about thirty minutes and was having another espresso when a thin, wiry man about twenty-five years old stepped in front of him, threw his leg over the chair and slid into the seat. He had a broad smile, a stubble of beard, and perfect white teeth. A cigarette dangled from the first two fingers of his left hand as he offered his right hand to shake Martin's.

"Good morning," the man said cheerily with only a trace of Italian accent. "I am Santo, and I understand you want to learn about the *Sassi*. Many men, they lived there for many centuries. Probably the first men to live in Italy. Even before the Greeks came here," he said.

According to Santo, the Romans settled the area in the 3rd century B.C., but it was overrun by the Lombards in the 7th century. During the Middle Ages, monks saw the caves up on the hill, saw that many people already lived there, and established monasteries among the *Sassi*. Over the next few centuries, the region was conquered by the Byzantines, Goths, Ostrogoths, Spanish Bourbons, the Normans, then the Germans during the war.

At this last comment, Martin blanched.

But Santo didn't notice his reaction so he continued. But after ten more minutes, Santo stopped suddenly, assuming his summary had impressed the visitor and would be enough to win the contract to guide Martin through the hills.

"*Signore, mi dispiace*," Santo said. "I'm so sorry. I talk so much and I don't even ask your name."

Martin expected this moment would come and he had considered offering a false name to avoid connection to Anselm Bernhard. But he knew that a deceit at this juncture might prove debilitating later in the relationship.

"It is Martin. Martin Bernhard."

"*Va bene*," Santo replied happily, "Signor Bernhard, it would be my pleasure to accompany you to the *Sassi* and tell you all that I know about them."

The guide excused himself from the table to report to his cousin, the waiter, that he would be leaving soon to take the young man on a tour of the caves. A whispered conversation occurred at the doorway to the kitchen, with the waiter pointing to Martin and Santo's expression turning from one of success to worried doubt. But he returned to the table with a broad smile on his lips.

"*Allora*," he began, "so, we go?"

"*Sì*," was Martin's reply. He worried a little that the conversation back in the doorway concerned his identity, but Santo seemed ready to proceed. Martin hoped to take advantage of this sliver of trust and complete his mission.

Chapter 24

Riding the Waves into Messina, September 3, 1943

By the summer of 1943, the Allied conquest of North Africa and invasion of Sicily seriously diminished the Fascist government's power. Mussolini had promised Italy greatness and expected to be the leader of a new Roman Empire, but his army's defeats undermined his support at home and reduced his government to puppet status, controlled by Hitler to maintain a military presence in Italy.

The Führer needed to keep Mussolini in power but the collapse of popular support for Il Duce *left even a weak King Vittorio Emanuele with little choice. On July 25, 1943, Mussolini was forced from power and later arrested. His replacement, Pietro Badoglio, was a man more inclined to accommodate the king and immediately began secret talks with the Allied forces to negotiate an armistice for Italy.*

Meanwhile, the British and American forces were racing to Messina with plans to cross the straits and make landfall on the shores of the Italian mainland to begin the march north. Field Marshall Bernard Montgomery led the British force and General George Patton commanded the Americans.

On September 3, 1943, as Montgomery's forces were landing in the toe of the Italian boot, Badoglio surrendered to the Allies, although the action was initially kept secret, in part because of the continued presence of large German military contingents throughout Italy. The peace agreement acknowledged the large German military occupation, but required the Badoglio government to assist the Allies in expelling the Nazi forces from Italy.

Chapter 25

An Afternoon in the Sassi

Martin slid into the passenger seat of Santo's car. He wasn't sure of the make or model. In fact, Martin thought the vehicle might even be a cannibalized version made of parts from several models. Of course there were no seat belts or air conditioning, but in his visits to Italy he had come to realize Italians didn't like air conditioning which they believed was bad for the joints and preferred to swelter in the heat of the summer.

Since arriving in Altamura, Martin had done little driving, so he didn't recognize the roads Santo took to escape the populated area, though he could tell by the sun that they were headed due south. They left the colorful views of the white-washed buildings and green gardens behind them, and they entered upon a parched land that stretched ahead of the car for miles.

Soon Martin saw the rise of the Murge ahead along with the contours of the Gravina riverbed. In a few more minutes, openings in the caves on the cliffs became more apparent. As they got closer, Martin began to pick out individual dwellings and some larger silhouettes that he assumed would be the churches and other communal caves that were part of the *Sassi* world.

Santo parked his car in a public parking lot at the base of the cliffs. Emerging from the heat of the cramped car, Martin surveyed the surroundings.

"How strange," Martin said referring to the newly paved parking lot. "I'm surprised to find such a modern convenience here."

"*Sì*, all the cars are parked here. The *Sassi* have attracted much attention in recent years, and tourists come. Like you!" Santo said to his guest.

He showed Martin the way to enter the neighborhood of the caves, then directed him down the paths that connected some of the most congested groupings. Every so often, Martin pulled the journal from his pocket and thumbed through the notes, looking at the groupings of caves around him as he did so.

Santo was intrigued with Martin's close inspection and asked what the book was about.

"Is this a guidebook to the *Sassi*?"

Martin quickly returned the journal to his pocket.

"No, no, it's just a book that has been in my family. It's about Italy. It's not important," he stammered.

Santo continued to think about the little book as they proceeded through various caves, but his running banter was now more sparse as his mind kept returning to Martin's journal.

The art collector focused on his surroundings, concerned that consulting Anselm's book again might raise more of Santo's suspicions. In fixing his attention on the caves, Martin began to understand the world's fascination with the *Sassi*. His memory wandered back to his research on the area, and to the books he had already read about the people of both the Murge and the *Sassi*. The descriptions of the area and its civilization from his books were echoed in Santo's explanations, and Santo's words and Martin's recollections merged into a long-running narrative on southern Italy, Matera and the *Sassi*, and the eons that civilization reigned in this area.

"Thousands of years ago Greeks settled in the southern part of our country, but old societies were already there," said Santo. "Caves were dug into the hillside of the Murge, safely placed to survive bad weather and hungry animals. By the time the Greeks got there, there was already a civilization of early Italians, people living alongside farm animals in the *Sassi*, sometimes not going down the slopes into the valley below for long stretches of time."

Martin knew that cisterns had been dug among the caves to catch rain water for the people there. In time, communal buildings snuggled in between the rude domestic caves; later still, wall painting and other adornments appeared, giving this strange rocky landscape a more developed, cultured feel.

Through thousands of years, the *Sassi* lived in the caves while civilization grew up in the area surrounding the Murge. Empires rose and fell, wars were fought and won – or lost – and still generation after generation lived in the *Sassi* and seemed likely to be there for all eternity.

"It wasn't until after World War II that the Italian government forced people to leave the *Sassi*," continued Santo. He explained that occasional bouts of poor health that sometimes resembled an epidemic in the caves were blamed on the living conditions there. Politically, the government was concerned that having people living in caves would make modern Italy seem primitive. Clearing the caves of human existence would erase that narrative.

In the 1950s, the government issued warnings, and then stepped up its efforts, demanding that the *Sassi* be evacuated.

But Martin realized that when his grandfather had visited this area in search of "great treasure," the *Sassi* would have still been occupied and its people could very well have been the custodians of the precious artifacts.

Martin emerged slowly from his reverie as Santo's voice reached his ears.

"This is the great Chiesa di Santa Maria d'Idris," he said, waving his hand toward the carved altar and paintings on the walls.

Martin was awed by the frescoes covering the walls of the church. Though faded, the original blue, pink, yellow, and orange hues were still visible, bringing to life scenes from the Old and New Testament. The characters depicted in some of the paintings would have been known only to the original inhabitants of these caves, but Martin glowed with excitement as he distinguished the elders who addressed assembled masses, the scenes of animal sacrifice, and portrayals of the souls rising into the heavens above.

As an art historian, he had focused on Renaissance art and could recognize a Michelangelo or a Botticelli painting from just a few square centimeters on a page, but these ancient paintings – made by a less talented artist but with similar devotion – reached out to the passion he had within him, the passion he once felt as an avid young art student at the university.

Unlike the great masterpieces that were typically commissioned by a rich or powerful patron, Martin knew that these paintings were rendered by simple people whose love of the *Sassi* and devotion to their religion were the only inspiration – and only payment. Martin approached the fresco on one wall and inspected the details of the composition. A broad staircase dominated the center of the painting, on which stood a man in long robes accompanied by a slightly shorter woman with flowing dark hair and wearing robes of yellow and pink, tied with a rope sash. The people gathered around them stood at the base of the steps but all pointed upward toward some destination that the couple was inclined toward.

Although he was impressed, he also had to admit that these old artworks were best appreciated from a distance, where the ravages of time and weather lost their affect and the whole of the composition could be taken in with a single glance.

He remembered entries in his grandfather's journal referring to a *kirche*, or church in the *Sassi*. This was one but he knew there would be others. Still, he couldn't resist drawing the book from his pocket to refresh his memory of Anselm's notes. Santo watched him closely, while Martin inspected the journal, as his eyes scanned the walls and then the floor, index finger pointing at one of the entries on the page.

They spent a few more moments in that church, then exited into the midday sunlight. Santo reached into his sack and drew out a water bottle, a loaf of bread, and another wrapped bundle. Pulling on the paper that enclosed it, Santo revealed a substantial hunk of meat that had been cooked with sage and olive oil, its scent quickly wafting toward Martin. Santo offered some of the repast to his guest.

"*No, grazie,*" came Martin's reply.

Santo shrugged his shoulders in the Italians' timeless gesture of "whatever," as he pulled hunks of bread from the loaf, washed down with great gulps of water.

Martin studied the journal again and found some vague references to churches, some with names and some without. The single word *versteckt* – hidden – appeared several times, but not in conjunction with other words or phrases, so he couldn't tell what his grandfather was trying to convey.

"What is that?" Santo asked again. "The old book of your family's?"

Santo spoke to him through bites of bread, something about other churches, and Martin realized that he was being a bit too obvious. He folded the book closed and returned it to his pocket.

"Yes," was Martin's only reply.

"So, your name is Bernhard," Santo continued.

Martin paused and then said, "Yes, my name is Martin Bernhard." He toyed with revealing that his grandfather had come to this area during the war, but decided against it.

"My cousin, he says he knows Bernhard," Santo said.

"Anselm Bernhard was my grandfather. He was an officer in the German army during the war."

"*Sì, sì,*" Santo said, nodding. "I know this. He was here during the war. My people remember him. He was not a good man."

A slight color rose up Martin's neck and into his cheeks, more from embarrassment than anger.

"But you are a good man," said Santo with raised eyebrows. At first, Martin took that as a compliment, but as Santo's eyes bore into him, he realized that the guide was asking him a question.

Martin swallowed hard, briefly looked down at his feet, and began his well-practiced speech about his grandfather.

"During the war, the Nazis did many terrible things, in this land and in others. We, the German people are not like them, we are ashamed that that evil empire ever arose from our culture. Anselm Bernhard was like many other decent Germans who got swept up in the fervor that was inspired by Hitler and the Third Reich. What they did wasn't right, but their actions didn't come from their own souls, they came from Hitler's threats and the actions of his henchmen."

"Decent," Santo repeated, focusing on a solitary word in Martin's narrative. "Anselm Bernhard was a decent man."

Martin squirmed. He knew too much about his grandfather's activities, the shameful thefts and more shameful attacks on Italian women that his grandmother had told him about. He used the word 'decent' to try to mitigate the blame cast on his entire family, but at the same time, he knew that his grandfather didn't deserve to be described so.

"You," Santo said, "you are a decent man?"

Martin nodded slightly, but refrained from putting up a defense of his grandfather.

Santo turned his attention back to the food and water he had in his hands, but eyed Martin more coldly than before. Shortly after, they resumed their tour of the *Sassi*, this time with fewer words spoken between them, and with Martin more reluctant than ever to draw the journal from his pocket.

As he studied the caves and surrounding area, they completed a brief tour after about another hour. There were too many caves and too many churches for Martin to continue in his quest in one afternoon. But this brief visit and general tour would give him ideas to contemplate later in the day, when he could peruse the journal in the privacy of his own room in Altamura.

Chapter 26

New Lessons

Carlo spent the morning at the bread ovens again under Zia Filomena's tutelage. The ladies gathered to bake bread were a generation older than their American visitor, but they had embraced him warmly, to the point of preening and sometimes embarrassing themselves.

"Carlo, do you want to knead my dough?" asked Lidia with a twinkle in her eye. Marta stood next to her but elbowed Lidia after that comment.

Carlo blushed lightly but took it kindly enough; at times he laughed at their jokes, knowing that these ladies were acting out an age-old drama in the human story between man and woman. The compliments are sometimes exaggerated, the jokes sometimes risque, but this is a part of relationships between the sexes that has played out in every society for centuries.

Zia Filomena gave him careful instruction on the shape and texture of the dough before it went into the oven. She passed her wrinkled hand close to the mouth of the fire-hot pit, even dipping her long fingers quickly into the opening to test the temperature. Not satisfied with the heat, Zia reached behind her for a long-handled wooden spade, poking it into the oven to rearrange the timbers that burned within. Smacking the paddle on the edge of the oven to cast off the embers, she tested the temperature again, nodded her head in a satisfied way, and turned toward Carlo.

"In your oven, at home, the temperature can be set by a dial. It's easy, *semplice,*" she said, "but the walls of your oven do not concentrate the heat like our stones do." Zia emphasized her comment by pointing to the rounded roof of the oven in front of her.

"Home baking won't produce the good bread, the bread that Altamura is known for." She smiled, nodding her head, "The bread that the spirit gives us."

Carlo knew that Zia Filomena and the other women at the oven – in fact, all the people of Altamura – used the term 'spirit' with more reverence than a simple reference to yeast. To them, the spirit moved the bread and wine and brought these products into being. He wondered whether the Chiesa dello Spirito Santo, the *Church of the Holy Spirit*, was named for their yeast, or the town's reference to the yeast came from the church.

In the afternoon, Giovanna took Carlo along on her rounds of shopping, first to the butcher shop and then the open air market for dinner that night. Many of the ingredients they used for cooking were grown in their small garden, but gardens couldn't grow pig and cow, nor could all the herbs necessary for an Italian repast be squeezed into the several square feet that Zia and Gia cultivated outside their home.

Carlo knew that Cristiano had a larger plot of land devoted to vines, but hadn't visited it yet.

"Why don't you command some of Cristiano's vineyard for your vegetables and herbs?" he asked Gia.

She laughed and shrugged her shoulders.

"The vineyard is on the edge of Altamura, too far from the house, so growing anything there would require too many trips back and forth."

That sounded like a perfect reason to Carlo, but then Giovanna added, "Anyway, could you imagine my father giving up some of his vines so mama and I could grow onions?"

Even a man dedicated to wine had to eat, Carlo thought, but he also knew that the vines were sacred to Cristiano. He chuckled at Gia's explanation, realizing that her father would never pull up a few vines when he knew that the women could manage with the plot they had near their home.

Walking back from the market, Carlo asked Giovanna to tell him more about the people he had met, including Don Adolfo, Nino, and the others that he met at church.

Every village has its rumors, secrets, and gossip, and these stories usually make for good conversation. So it didn't take long for Gia to dip into the tales of Sofina and Nino, and life in the convent.

"Nino was born in the convent." With this startling beginning, she had Carlo's full attention.

"He is the bastard son of Sofina who lived in the convent. She was brought there *incinta,* 'pregnant,' during the war. Nino was born there and spent his first few years among the nuns, tended by his mother. But when he was about ten years old, it was no longer fitting for him to stay among the women living in the convent. Sofina tearfully agreed to have him live with the Cantone family, where he grew up.

"He remained very quiet in the convent. Some people say it was the environment there that stole his tongue. *Forse,*" she said with a shrug. "Maybe. But he never really found it afterward. He has remained very quiet, 'a man of few words' as you Americans say, his whole life."

"He was born during the war?" Carlo repeated. "So he's about seventy?"

"*Sì, sì.* He grew up with the Cantones but visited his mother every day and made himself useful by fixing things and doing chores for the nuns. He became very skilled with tools and machines, and Don Adolfo asked him to help also around the *Chiesa.*

"Sofina died long ago, when he was still a young man, about twenty-five."

Carlo did some quick math and assumed Sofina had died about 1970.

"Was she a nun?" he asked.

"Oh, no," said Gia emphatically, shaking her head. "Her sin was too great to become a nun. She never took the vows or wore the habit; but she lived among the nuns until her death. Sofina was also a very skilled person, but her skills were with the garden."

Carlo listened intently, nodding his head.

"The sisters said that Sofina could grow anything," Giovanna continued, "and anything she grew was the best, the sweetest fruit, the most beautiful flowers, the biggest vegetables. They said the ground she tilled was blessed."

Gia paused for a moment, considering her next words.

"But how can she be blessed," Carlo interrupted, "She has an illegitimate child!"

"Sex makes babies, and not all Italians are virgins." She made this last comment with widened eyes.

"But having a baby, well that part is hard to hide," she added. "The church says we shouldn't have sex, but no one is listening to that part of the sermon. Some of the people in Altamura think it's not that Sofina had sex, or even that she had a baby, but it's who the father is that made her so ashamed."

Chapter 27

Altamura, September 7, 1943

The German convoy rumbled into Altamura in the late afternoon. Stepping out of the Kübelwagen, Bernhard put his hands on his hips and surveyed the piazza. He spun left then right, looking at the buildings that framed the square. His scrutiny was bold and possessive; it didn't take much for the townspeople to realize he was looking for the best home to seize for his personal use.

Lace curtains were drawn; doors slammed shut. A little boy in a tattered shirt stood outside one shop, too young to be afraid of this invading force, until he was yanked inside by his frightened mother.

Bernhard sneered at the attempts to shut him out. "Italians," he said with undisguised contempt.

"Hilgendorf," he commanded, and pointing to a stone house in front of him. "Go in there and see what it's like. If you approve, come find me and I'll see if I agree." Then spinning on his left heel, he added, "I'll be at the café."

The junior officer let himself in through the front door, with only a slight nod to the occupants and with little ceremony or respect for their privacy.

The home was much like what they had seen in other Italian towns. Plain on the outside, but reasonably elegant within, even in this small southern town. Skillfully carved wooden furniture filled the rooms, lace curtains were mounted above heavy glass windows, and etched pitchers and glasses sat upon the table that was set for supper.

Hilgendorf didn't carry himself with the arrogance of his commanding officer, but he didn't wait for the woman of the house to invite him into the other rooms. Ducking his head to clear the low doorway, he stepped into each of the four other rooms in the house. There were two bedrooms neatly kept, a sitting room with an ancient radio that looked as if it was one of the first invented. In the kitchen Hilgendorf was surrounded by the aromas of a freshly made minestrone and loaf of fragrant bread just out of the oven.

"This will do," he said to no one in particular. By now, the woman's husband had been summoned and the couple stood stock still in the parlor waiting for the lieutenant to complete his survey. Hilgendorf addressed the couple in clipped Italian phrases learned as a schoolboy in Germany.

"Colonel Bernhard needs this house. You will need to leave."

The man looked at him in disbelief, then turned to his wife. "Che cos'é?" he asked, with a look that mixed grief, anger, and incredulity." The woman laid her hand lightly on his arm to calm him. She didn't nod or shake her head, but she peered intently into her husband's eyes, telling him with her silent reply that this German's words were not a request.

The man looked back at the intruder with an expression that showed more anger than grief, but his wife squeezed his arm firmly to stop him from saying anything.

"You should go now," said Hilgendorf, knowing that he had to move these people along quickly before the confrontation turned ugly. Waving his hand toward the woman, he added, "But you will stay. Your supper is almost ready and the colonel is hungry."

Hilgendorf marched out the door to notify his commander that the house was acceptable and that his next meal would be served soon.

After inspecting the house himself, Bernhard agreed that the premises would suit his needs well, and he invited Hilgendorf to take supper with him. After eating, the colonel cordially thanked the woman for serving his dinner, reminded her that he ate three times a day and that he would expect her to continue to feed him, but the rest of the time she should absent herself from the premises.

Following the meal, Bernhard stepped toward the broad window facing the piazza below. He drew the curtains back and opened the window, lighting a cigar as he did so. With Hilgendorf, the two men looked out over the piazza and observed that the other German soldiers in the detachment had settled into tables at the café for their wine and food.

"Is it true about the Italians surrendering?" Hilgendorf asked. He knew the question would not be welcome, but his relationship with the higher officer gave him more latitude to ask such things than the other soldiers had.

Bernhard didn't answer, but continued puffing on his cigar.

Hilgendorf turned toward the colonel and asked again. "The men have heard rumors, rumors that Mussolini has been thrown out of power and the new guy, what's his name – Badoglio? – has surrendered. Is it true?"

Without looking at the lieutenant, Bernhard blew out a long stream of thick smoke between pursed lips. "So, maybe, but that doesn't concern us."

"If the Italians have surrendered, aren't we in a dangerous place?" the young officer asked. "We're in the south, very far from the German border. How can we escape if the Italians and the Americans surround us?"

Again, Bernhard didn't answer.

Hilgendorf turned back toward the piazza and listened to the soldiers' laughter below. They didn't seem concerned at that moment, but when they brought their rumors to him in the afternoon, several of them had been ready to argue that they should quit the mission and return to the Fatherland. Hilgendorf agreed that this was probably the right thing to do, but he also knew that Bernhard's obsession with this new fortune he'd heard about would override his men's fears of capture.

Hilgendorf waited in silence for a few more moments, hoping the colonel would add something, but he didn't. After a while, the lieutenant turned and left the apartment.

After another moment, as Bernhard puffed on his cigar, he noticed a young woman walking across the piazza below. Her long hair and con-

fident stride convinced him at once that this was Marisa. He enjoyed the view for a moment then decided to walk out to the piazza.

The woman of the house was washing the supper dishes, but Bernhard exited the apartment without even looking at her.

* * *

Marisa never looked at the house that Bernhard occupied. In fact, she had spied him from the edge of the piazza before beginning her seductive walk past the cafés. She knew where he was and she knew he would see her when she passed by, and follow her.

Chapter 28

Café Rosato

After a sumptuous dinner that Carlo had come to expect from Zia Filomena and her daughter, Gia took him to the piazza to find Arabella. After spotting her at a table, Gia and Carlo joined her.

"*Vino rosso?*" Arabella asked, raising her glass.

"*Sì, sì, perfetto,*" was Giovanna's ready response.

The conversation proceeded easily and covered topics familiar to the young women.

"Bianca is now working at the dress shop," said Arabella. "Her mother doesn't like it, says that there was no reason to go to the university 'if you're only going to make aprons,' she says." Both of the girls laughed at this, knowing that Bianca got her degree to please her parents, but they also knew that the young lady's hands could make beautiful magic with even homespun fabrics.

Gia sipped some wine, held the glass up to the light, and thought for a moment. Signaling the waiter, she requested a plate of sweets and biscotti for them to share.

"Too much wine, too little food," she commented with a small laugh.

Carlo contributed only occasionally, preferring to sit and enjoy the company. Gia had become like a sister to him since he was living in her house, but Arabella intrigued him.

Her light hair appeared darker in the fading sunlight, but the brightness of her blue eyes was still alluring. Her voice reminded him of a trained actress's talent to use her voice to evoke different moods. Gia laughed at Arabella's story about the car that swept past her on the sidewalk that morning, and Gia added her own story of slipping between the teeming traffic on her way to the school.

Carlo knew that Gia tutored children at the local school and could not join them at the ovens that morning. Her stories of the kids' behavior made Arabella laugh, and Carlo was able to observe and appreciate the spirit that bound these two women together.

Arabella turned to Carlo to include him in the conversation.

"So you are learning to bake our famous *Pane di Altamura*."

"Well, yes," he said. "I'm learning, but I doubt I could duplicate it yet."

"Well, you never will," said Giovanna, "because the spirit of Altamura is only here."

They turned to the subject of the "spirit in the air," the yeast cells that populate the areas they have already been propagated in, like the kitchens where the dough is prepared, the oven where the bread is baked, and even the small home wineries where the grapes are turned into wine. Carlo knew enough about winemaking to know that natural yeast clings to the ripening grapes in the field, and that unless you introduce something more specific and artificial, it is this yeast strain that will determine the path of the fermentation and the flavors in the final wine.

"Everyone here talks about the 'spirit' as if there is something in the air that makes the bread and wine so good," he said.

The two women looked at him as if waiting for him to say more.

"Of course there's something in the air," said Arabella finally. Her look conveyed her confusion.

"No, I mean the yeast," he retorted.

Giovanna let out a little huff of exasperation. "Well, *sì*, there's the yeast, but the spirit is with us in Altamura. That's why our church is named *dello Spirito*."

Carlo studied her and then Arabella. He wasn't sure whether they had simply translated the scientific explanation of yeast through metaphor to a sentient 'spirit,' but he had run into this before in Altamura. The people of this town were smart people and they knew that yeast cells initiated and prolonged fermentation, but they also were adamant about the 'spirit in the air' being something more than simple yeast cells.

"For many years, Altamura has been a blessed place," said Arabella. "We are rewarded with our comfortable lives, our culture, and our beliefs. We are watched over by a special spirit that protects us from evil."

Gia chimed in. "Ever since the war, when people from around the southern regions of Italy brought us their treasures, we have lived in the grace of God."

This was the first time Carlo had heard of treasures in Altamura, but he noticed that a stranger sitting at the next table had suddenly turned in their direction.

"Excuse me," said the man, "did you say something about treasure in Altamura?"

Gia and Arabella regarded Martin suspiciously. Strangers asking about riches residing in their town made them nervous. Arabella spoke first.

"*Sì*, that's what we said, but there are no treasures here." She then turned back around to their table and tried to ignore Martin.

"I am an art collector, and I have specialized in the art of Italy. I would be very interested in knowing more about art, gems, or other valuables that may be in Altamura."

Giovanna and Arabella looked at each other but didn't respond. Carlo was the one to break the silence.

"My name is Carlo de Vito," he said, rising to offering his hand to shake. Martin took it, and then introduced himself.

"You are not from here," Carlo continued.

"No, I am German. I work at the Institute of Renaissance Art in Berlin and, like I said, I am especially interested in Italian art."

Gia then whispered something to Arabella. Their conspiratorial tone cut the men's conversation off. Martin thanked Carlo for his thoughts and turned back toward his own table.

"Very interesting career, art history, that is," Carlo said.

Gia glared at him. "You know who that is, right?" Carlo shook his head 'no.'

Arabella sighed, then explained to Carlo. "He is Bernhard, the grandson of the man who stole our property, raped our women, and killed our priest, Don Daniele, when he was here in 1943."

"How do you know that?" Carlo asked.

"This is a small town, and we are a close community," Gia said. "He clerk at the hotel told some friends that a man named Bernhardt was here, asking about art," she added with a huff. "This Bernhard says he's an art collector, but maybe he just wants to 'collect' the rest of art that his *nonno* didn't get a chance to steal!"

Martin remained at the table behind her and he could clearly hear her words. He was shocked and embarrassed, but Arabella's passion kept him silent.

"What treasure?" Carlo asked.

"Never mind," said Arabella.

"No," added Gia, "not just never mind. There has been talk of such things for many years, but no one has found it."

"But, what is it?" asked Carlo again.

Gia shrugged her shoulders, and Arabella remained silent.

Martin slid his chair out noiselessly, stood, and walked out of the café.

Casting a glance over her shoulder at the German, Gia said, "He's a bastard. All the Nazis were bastards."

"Yes," Carlo said calmly, hoping to offer some words to defuse the tension. "The Nazis were bastards, but he's not a Nazi. He's from Germany, sure, but the German people are ashamed of that era. This guy seems nice enough..."

"Nice? Nice enough?" Gia blurted out. The bitterness that showed in her voice surprised Carlo, and he sat back in his chair.

Arabella patted Gia on the arm to calm her, but then Arabella took up the argument.

"He is Bernhard, the man who did horrible things to Altamura."

"No, he's not that Bernhard," said Carlo.

Arabella looked away, using her palm to wipe away tears that began streaming down her cheek. "He's the same. They're all the same."

Chapter 29

Nothing

Tempers had cooled by the next day. Gia even apologized to Carlo but reminded him that they would have nothing to do with the German.

About mid-morning, Arabella picked them up in her car for some sightseeing. Carlo had asked about the *Sassi* and the plateau known as the Murge, and the two women decided it would be a nice day for a tour.

On the brief ride to the cliffs, Arabella and Giovanna told stories about the people who lived in the *Sassi* and how the civilization in the caves had flourished for many centuries. They also talked about the lifestyle of the people, how the homes had been modernized over the years and how the Italian government had evacuated the dwellings in the 1950s.

"Today there is renewed interest in the *Sassi*," said Gia. It was declared a UNESCO World Heritage Site and, suddenly, the Italian government decided that the caves are not so bad after all." Both women laughed at this.

"Why are you laughing?" Carlo wondered.

"The government decided after the war that people living in caves didn't represent the kind of modern society that they were trying to build in Italy. So they forced people to leave," said Gia.

"Now," continued Arabella, "they think cave dwelling is good for our local economy, so they're telling people to move back in!"

"Well," Giovanna said, "not exactly. The government has allowed some tourism agencies to rebuild the caves as hotels and restaurants. It's pretty good, actually, but there won't be a civilization like the *Sassi* again."

When they arrived at the caves, the women conducted a tour that they were very familiar with, introducing Carlo to the homes, churches, and communal areas of the *Sassi*. They told him how people lived, how they survived, and how they extended the complex labyrinth of caves throughout the mountain.

"What about the treasure?" Carlo asked.

Both women stopped their running narrative to look at Carlo.

"There is no treasure," Arabella said patiently. "There were rumors of this here, in Altamura, and the Germans thought they could find it and steal it from us. The Germans, like Anselm Bernhard."

"But there really wasn't any treasure," Gia said. "He tore up many of the caves, broke up the stone altars in some of the churches, and scattered the people who lived there, forcing them to move into other caves, while he ransacked their homes.

"What did he find?" asked Carlo.

"*Nulla,*" was Arabella's terse reply. "Nothing," she said again, the pain causing her voice to crack.

Chapter 30

Back to Café Rosato

Carlo was on his own that evening, as Gia had more tutoring to do and Zia Filomena stayed at home to help Cristiano with some chores.

He was drawn to the piazza where most of the people spent their evenings, and spied Martin Bernhard sitting alone at a café table. Carlo decided that the man deserved a chance, so he approached his table.

Martin had been badly hurt by the women's treatment the previous day, and he recognized Carlo as their acquaintance, so he was reluctant to engage him in additional conversation.

"May I sit down?"

With a long sigh, Martin nodded yes.

"You said you are an art collector. That's very interesting; could you tell me more about your work?"

Martin brightened a little at Carlo's approach, and he launched into an excited narrative about his education, his work, and the trips he had made to Italy to find and restore old artworks to their rightful owners. At one point, he bowed his head when he realized that further discussion would require that he return to the subject of his grandfather, but Carlo had been attentive and seemed to appreciate Martin's mission.

"I lived my whole life not knowing what my grandfather had done," Martin began. He was staring at his hands folded on the table before him. "A few years ago, my grandmother was dying, and she told me of the evil things that Anselm had done, the way he treated the Italian people, the way he mistreated the Italian women.

"And she gave me his journal," he added. "I had never heard anything about this, and I knew nothing of a journal. But my grandmother asked me – no, made me promise – to restore our honor by making reparation for his awful deeds."

He looked at Carlo, his eyes expressing both resolve and shame.

"I can't do anything for the women that he violated, and I can't find all the art that he looted, but I have found some and restored them. As I promised my grandmother."

"Why are you here?" Carlo asked.

"In his journal, my grandfather had many notes about a great collection, one valuable beyond imagining, hidden in a town in southern Italy. He spoke of caves and churches, and there were some notes that indicated that he had been to Altamura."

"Obviously," said Carlo and, with that, Martin understood that everyone here knew that Anselm had been to Altamura.

"Yes, obviously," he said with resignation.

"But that doesn't explain why you are here," persisted Carlo. "You said you are trying to find the artifacts, the collections, that your grandfather stole and restore them to their rightful owners, right?"

Martin nodded.

"Well, if he never found what he was looking for, here in Altamura...why are you here?"

Martin's mind wandered back to the evening spent at home, when he had explained to Margrit the purpose of his many trips to Italy. And he recalled with some shame his own thoughts while standing alone at the window of the study. He was pure in his desire to make amends for his grandfather's crimes, but the thought of undiscovered treasure raised the hair on his neck and forced him to confront dark hints of his own greed.

Martin had not put it in such words, but he had to admit that Carlo's challenge was a strong one. From the time he received Anselm's journal, he had wondered about the treasure of Altamura. And while he searched throughout Italy for other stolen goods, returning some to the grandchildren of the original Italian families who owned them, he contemplated the great mystery surrounding the artworks and gems that his grandfather sought here in the south. But if Anselm had not found that great fortune, and the absence of any record of such a find in the journal suggested that he had not, Martin couldn't completely resolve his own obsession with Altamura either.

Had he inherited his ancestor's wickedness?

"In my research," Martin replied, "I studied the Monuments Men, a unit made up of American and British soldiers, and some French, whose responsibility was to prevent damage to art works and monuments during the war, the Second World War. They were in the battlefield, sometimes ahead of the fighting, trying to identify these artifacts and historic buildings and rope them off so the fires of war wouldn't consume them.

"The onslaught of military fighting threatened these so-called 'monuments,' but the unit didn't think about the theft and damage that my German predecessors had already committed – the priceless paintings and sculptures that the German army had already absconded with.

"One of the Monuments Men wrote to his wife back in the States: 'The Germans have behaved very badly, and in the last days of their occupation, savagely. From here, now, they do not look like a simple innocent people with criminal leaders. They look like criminals. And I wonder how long it will take to get them to live fairly with the rest of the world.'

"I am of the next generation of Germans," Martin continued, "and I am trying to live fairly with the rest of the world by making amends for sins of my fathers. How long will it take?"

Chapter 31

Dinner with Arabella

Their conversation stumbled a bit after that, but returned to simpler subjects when Martin asked why Carlo was in Altamura.

"I am an Italian-American. I live in St. Louis, and we were raised to respect the Italian traditions. But St. Louis is so far from here, and I wanted to learn more about true Italian life. A friend introduced me to the Filomena family, and they agreed to host me for a few weeks while I learned more about life in southern Italy." He laughed a bit and then admitted to Martin that he was also learning to make bread.

Martin laughed. "To make bread?"

"Yes, well, I would like to learn more about it, and besides, I'm also learning to make wine. But my real reason for coming to Altamura was to learn to live like an Italian, to understand why they think the way they do, and to try to understand how I think and how my family thinks, and to come to terms with how Italian life and culture has affected my life."

"That's a big quest," said Martin. "And I thought I was the only one looking for great treasure!"

Both men laughed and continued a light conversation that covered their preferences in food, wine, college education, and the politics of their respective countries. Without returning to the painful memories of his grandfather's life in Italy, Martin explained that he had come to love the country and its people.

"I studied Italian in school. Many of the German children do that, or learn some other foreign language, but the sound and rhythm of the Italian language intrigued me," he explained. "I'm not particularly good at it. I can understand more than I can pronounce myself, but it's good enough.

"Italians are passionate and warm-hearted," Martin continued. "They accept each other and newcomers equally, and I have always felt welcome when I visited the cities across the country." With some introspection, he added, "But mostly in the northern part of Italy."

Carlo furrowed his brow, trying to understand what point Martin was trying to make.

"The northerners are more accustomed to us Germans, Swiss, and other Europeans. The south is more insular, more protective."

"And poorer," added Carlo.

"Yes, poorer. And maybe the economy affects their traditions, their beliefs, and their outlook on the world. Southern Italy is more rural, more agricultural, than the north. And life is lived closer to the edge..."

"And closer to the earth," suggested Carlo.

"That too. And maybe given their history of invasions and exploitation, the southern Italians are more suspicious of outsiders. They don't trust us as much."

Carlo kept his thoughts to himself, but he didn't doubt the warm reception he got when he arrived. So Martin's conclusion that the southerners were less trusting of outsiders seem to relate to him, not Carlo.

They talked until the liter of wine was gone. Martin said he had to return to his hotel room. He rose, shook Carlo's hand, and departed.

Carlo sat there for another moment, replaying their conversation. He still had some wine left in his glass, another robust Primitivo that was so common in this area, and sipped at it slowly while he considered what his German friend had said.

"Do you always drink alone?"

Carlo looked up and smiled broadly at Arabella. She was a beautiful sight and he quickly rose to offer her a chair.

Arabella arrived in the piazza after Martin was long gone. Carlo decided it was best not to say who he had been talking to before her arrival. Instead, he pitched his questions about Italian culture to this lovely woman seated across from him.

"My family is from Toritto, and Palo del Colle, not far from here," he began. "So we are from the Mezzogiorno, like you. But we are different."

"Different? From us?"

"No," he laughed. "Different from other Italians."

"*Sì, un po',*" she nodded, "a bit, but not that much. Italians have always been special people, and you're right that the people of the north seem too European, and the people of the south seem, well, what do I say, too Italian."

Carlo laughed, enjoying her inability to describe her tribe as anything but the true Italian.

"In my research," he explained, "I learned that most of the Italians who came to America were from the south. In the time from 1880 to 1920 – well, more than that, but that was the primary time – millions of Italians flooded into the United States. Nearly all of them were from the south."

"*Sì,* it's true," Arabella offered. "But this is because the people of the Mezzogiorno are – well, were – very poor. During that time, there were famines, droughts, and continued insulation from the governing north, and we didn't have anything to hope for. We left, we went to South America and the United States, looking for jobs to feed and clothe our families."

Carlo noticed that Arabella spoke of the immigrants from southern Italy as 'we,' as if the time nearly a century ago was being lived by the people of Altamura even today.

"Is it true that, in America, Italian food is all pasta, sauce, and pizza?" she asked.

Carlo couldn't completely contain a chuckle.

"Not altogether. Yes, the Italian food that Americans first discovered was like that, but now we have learned to make better Italian food, more varied, with seafood, beef, truffles, and more."

"Hmmm," Arabella hummed. "But the pasta, sauce, and pizza...these are the foods of the Mezzogiorno. Americans discovered Italian food by eating the favorite things of our people."

"*Sì,*" Carlo responded. "The first Italian food in the U.S. was more like the south prepares." He wanted to repeat his assertion that Americans have become more sophisticated in their taste for Italian food, but he realized that this wasn't what Arabella wanted to hear, so he kept silent.

She sat quiet for a moment, seemingly absorbed with the notion that her culture and its food were America's first acquaintance with the land of her birth.

"This is good," she said after a bit of time had passed. She took a sip of wine and nodded. "This is good," but Carlo knew she was applauding the influence of the Mezzogiorno on America, not the ruby liquid that slid down her throat.

Chapter 32

Armistice, September 8, 1943

Church bells tolled with great animation, even though it was not an hour when the bells normally rang out. Conversations were just as animated, whether at the café in the piazzas and town halls in many Italian towns, or on the highways where cars had clustered at the roadside restaurants as their drivers argued about what they had heard.

An armistice between the Italian government led by the Italian general Pietro Badoglio and the Allied forces had been announced.

Before this day such a development was unthinkable. But since the dismissal of Mussolini, rumor had it that the Italian government had been negotiating with the Americans and the British to surrender. On this glorious day in early September, the deal that had been kept hidden from the public was finally announced.

Italy was free from the German yoke. Free, but not unencumbered. There were many regiments of the Third Reich still in Italy and the Badoglio government had agreed to cooperate with the Allied forces in driving them out. So a country that had surrendered to the invading army of Allies must now contend with the anger of occupying German forces.

* * *

Back in Altamura, the German soldiers crowded around Hilgendorf as Bernhard entered the room. Their whispered comments were suddenly

112

squelched, and the colonel proceeded past them into the room he was using as a command center.

Just behind their commanding officer, Marisa emerged from the same doorway. But unlike the colonel, she approached the men with a smile, making friendly talk, and teasing them about their uniforms and sidearms, artfully playing the seductress with her compliments and light touches on the arm of a few men.

Soon, one of the soldiers spoke to her in a stage whisper.

"It's true, isn't it? The Italians have surrendered."

Marisa follow such events closely and was quite certain that the news was true. Just as she was certain that these men had been led into a deadly trap by their own commander.

"Sì, it is true." But she didn't try to console them. She continued her innocent flirting, secretly focusing on their comments and concerns. After a while, she returned to the conversation.

"Colonel Bernhard told me that you are almost finished with the mission," she said. Marisa emphasized the "almost" to remind the soldiers that their colonel was not yet ready to leave the area.

"Almost finished?" said one of the soldiers. "We must leave now!"

Hilgendorf could sense the rising mutiny but stayed silent, trying to gauge what he could say and yet remain neutral.

Another soldier chimed in, "It is very dangerous here. I don't want to die with an American bullet in my back."

"Why in the back?" asked Marisa. "Why turn your backs and run? Besides, Herr Colonel says it's not time to leave." She paused for affect. "I don't think you'll ever be able to leave until he says so."

She knew that Bernhard's obsession with the secret treasure would make it impossible for him to pull the detachment out and head north to safety. And she suspected that the soldiers were also coming to that opinion.

The Germans began muttering words of hinted rebellion and vengeful murder. At one point the suggestions became so violent that Hilgendorf excused himself from the group.

*Marisa smiled, knowing that the soldiers were beginning to see Alta-
mura as their last stand, unless their colonel could be convinced to leave.
Or until they solved the problem themselves.*

*Surrounded by angry men muttering treasonous words, Marisa let her
thoughts drift back to the night before. She had maintained her role as the
seductress, even as Bernhard laid his hands upon her body, and she smiled
derisively at his self-congratulatory love making. When the colonel had
fallen into a deep sleep, Marisa padded softly around the bedroom looking
for a gun to silence the bastard once and for all. She knew the sound of
the gun's report would alert the neighbors, but they would protect her.
And given her afternoon ploy with the German soldiers, she didn't expect
them to arrest her.*

*Marisa slipped her hands under Bernhard's uniform jacket handing on
the door. Finding no weapon there, she sifted through his clothing stacked
neatly in the campaign chest at the foot of the bed. A rustle from the bed
clothes froze her in her quest, but Bernhard's labored snorts convinced
her that he was still asleep.*

*Marisa stood to survey the room and consider her alternatives. There
were knives in the kitchen, but she feared an attack that might not be
completely successful at first moment. She couldn't bear to let him slip
from her assault and be undone herself, dying before she could complete
the revenge of her sister's demise. As she peered around the room once
more, a whispered voice awoke her senses.*

"What are you doing?"

*It was Bernhard. He was propped up on both elbows and staring di-
rectly at her. His pillow had moved slightly and, from beneath it, Marisa
saw the slight glint of metal from under the pillowcase. The metal was
from Bernhard's sidearm. No wonder she hadn't found his weapon. The
Nazi was well aware of his own treacherous deeds and slept with only one
weapon in the vicinity, and that one tucked carefully beneath his head.*

*"Oh, nulla," she said with voice as soothing as she could muster. Then
she pulled back the cover and slipped between the sheets, shuddering in
an almost imperceptible way as Bernhard laid his hand upon her naked
thigh.*

Chapter 33

Piazza Veneto

The day was sunny and bright in Altamura. People walked about or drove their cars through the streets as they began the day's activities. The piazza was crowded, as always in towns such as this one, and many waves and greetings were exchanged.

Carlo had just left Zia Filomena at the ovens. He felt that he had learned enough for that day and wanted to explore more of the town before joining Cristiano in his small winery beside their home. He walked down the street, entered the piazza, and crossed over to the café to get an espresso. Carlo liked the morning atmosphere in Italy. The storekeepers rose with the sun, swept off the sidewalks outside their shops, and the smell of roasted coffee beans and sweet rolls filled the air.

In the morning hours, there were more lively conversations to start the day. In midday and the afternoon, most Italians concentrated their energy on the job or jobs at hand, and didn't return to their social conviviality until the *cena* – or supper – and then afterward during the *passeggiata* in the town square.

But in the crisp air of the morning, Carlo liked being surrounded by the subtler sounds of an Italian city, the smells of fresh bread and coffee, and the clear blue of the skies above. It was at that time that he felt more connected to Altamura than he had to other cities he visited in his ancestral land.

As he reached the opposite side of the piazza, Carlo saw a middle aged man he did not know. The man was talking to Martin and, although he couldn't yet hear the words that were exchanged, Carlo could tell from the unrestrained hand gestures that there was an argument underway.

Approaching the men, Carlo listened more closely.

"The Germans killed my uncle and my aunt. You're murderers," he said to Martin.

The art collector stood by, turning red in the face, but trying very hard not to engage the conversation.

"Bastardo!" repeated the man, several times. "Hell has your grandfather, and he awaits you there!"

Carlo was worried that this verbal onslaught would become worse, yet he was reluctant to become involved. At one point, Martin saw him standing just out of range, his eyes pleading for some intervention, but Carlo demurred.

The man continued the attack, pointing his finger at Martin and, at times, striking him in the chest. Occasionally, Martin had a reply, tried hard to remain patient and understanding, but acted as though he felt violated by the attack.

Carlo waited until the man had exhausted his venom then watched him walk away. Martin's shoulders had long since slumped into a victim's pose, and Carlo looked him over from head to toe.

There was no way to recover from the blitz of verbal abuse, and Carlo had nothing to offer in consolation. He looked once more at Martin, who returned his glance plaintively, and then Carlo turned and walked away.

Later in the morning, he felt guilty for abandoning the German so easily, but he had to admit that the people of Altamura had some very strong feelings about the way the Nazi troops had treated them seventy years before, and no words of wisdom from Carlo were going to change that.

Chapter 34

Life in Altamura

Carlo had grown fond of Arabella and wanted to see if she would agree to spend more time with him. When he had the chance, he asked her to join him for dinner at one of the *trattorie* in the town. 'A date' the Americans would have called it and, although Arabella understood the evening to represent the same purpose, she demurely pretended it to be just another opportunity to get to know the man and his culture in the United States.

"My uncles, they moved to America," she said over a plate of *lanache di casa,* tagliatelle dressed with mussels stuffed with breadcrumbs, eggs, and pecorino cheese, and stewed in a rich tomato sauce.

"Really? When was that?"

"Well, Zio Alberto left about fifteen years ago to follow his brother, Giusto. They found jobs in New York. Didn't like it at first, too crowded and noisy, but the money was good."

"Where are they now?" Carlo asked.

"They're still in New York. The money they can make there is so much more than here. They send money back to their families, and they're saving it up to buy more land outside of Altamura."

"Will they come back?"

"That's the plan." Arabella's fork dug into the tagliatelle and lifted a morsel into her mouth.

After a few moments of silent eating, they resumed.

"So many southern Italians who went to America a hundred years ago..." Carlo began.

"*Sì, sì*, they came back to Italy," she interrupted him.

"Yes, they did," he agreed. "They came back to Italy but most of them returned to America once more. They settled there. And that's why the United States had many millions of Italian immigrants and today has millions and millions of their Italian-American children and grandchildren."

Arabella considered this for a moment. "Times are different now."

"In what way?"

"In those days, there was no work here, I mean <u>no</u> work," she emphasized. "The men who went to America came back with their paychecks and stories of life in the New World. Unfortunately, the stories lasted longer than those paychecks did."

With a sigh, she added, "So they went back. They used the money they brought home to Italy to buy passage for their wives and children to move to America."

A long moment passed before anything else was said.

"Do you ever think of moving to America?" Carlo asked.

"No. Like I said, times have changed. The economy here is still not strong, but we are happy. My world is Altamura."

When Carlo considered her comments, Arabella asked, "Do you ever think of moving to Italy?"

He resisted the too-quick 'of course not' reply, sensing that he needed to be a bit more diplomatic. Carlo had to admit that he loved Italy and its people, and he was coming to respect the Altamurans like Arabella and the Filomena family, but he couldn't imagine leaving his home in St. Louis forever.

"No, I haven't thought about that. I guess I am connected to my home like you are connected to yours."

"*Sì*," she said looking into her glass of wine. "It is the home, but not just the place. It's the history, the traditions, the customs, the comfort we get from knowing when we wake up in the morning what the day will feel like, what we expect to experience when we kneel before God in our church, what we look forward to tasting when we take a seat at a *trattoria* such as this.

"Why would I leave?" Arabella concluded. Then, with a slight smile, she added, "Maybe it's the spirit in the air."

Chapter 35

Invasion of Italy, September 8, 1943

On the heels of the public announcement that Italy had reached an agreement with the Allies, American forces crossed over the Straits of Messina from Sicily to the toe of Italy. The British forces were already there to greet them and, with the additional armaments and troops, the Allies began a concerted effort to push on to the mainland.

Fighting could be heard throughout the southern tip of Italy and it moved steadily up into the region of Basilicata around Matera and Altamura. The Germans were being routed from all standing positions, and the Nazi forces were being squeezed between the advancing Allied forces and the Italian partisans on their northern frontier.

Many of the occupying German forces were pulling back, but some detachments remained to protect their flank except for Bernhard and his men who remained in Altamura to continue the search for the hidden riches in the Sassi.

Hilgendorf fielded many angry comments from the troops over a short twenty-four hour period. He, too, wanted to flee, but his sense of duty caused him to stay at Bernhard's side in the hope of convincing his superior officer to leave Italy.

Marisa was also staying close to Bernhard, in a much more intimate way than his lieutenant, but she was also talking to his discontented troops during those tense hours. She coyly took the colonel's side while still providing fodder for his troops' seditious talk. But to the soldiers she also seemed to be something of a war victim herself, cooperating with a man for survival. The Germans went to bed that night with the sound of cannon fire ringing in their ears, not certain if they would live until morning.

Early the next day, Marisa knew she had whipped the soldiers into a fearful frenzy. As the men stood about the café sipping hot coffee and talking, she slipped among them, putting on a tearful façade for the first time.

"What is wrong, Marisa?" one of the soldiers asked.

"Nothing," she said tersely. But the men looked on with concern and her questioner pressed her for more. They were careful to remember that she was their commander's consort, but they also detected a vulnerability in Marisa, an impression that she was adept at promoting.

Slowly, Marisa acted out the scene that she had prepared the night before for this very confrontation. She mentioned that Bernhard had been brusque with her. She pretended to excuse his behavior, saying the colonel was just as worried about the Americans as his troops were. But then...

Tearing up, she added, "He was rough with me. I know he's scared, but..." and with that, she rubbed her left cheek as if trying to erase the pain of being slapped, "he was not a gentleman to me."

The soldiers' talk turned to uglier things after that. Mistreating this woman who had befriended them was out of line. One man remained silent, but his eyes burned with an intensity that Marisa welcomed.

Hilgendorf tried to calm the men while their voices rose – all but the one soldier who kept his silence, staring at the ground in front of him.

Chapter 36

Back to the Sassi

Later that morning, Bernhard barked an order to Hilgendorf.

"We're returning to the caves today. We need to continue our mission."

Marisa stood nearby, as did some of the soldiers in the detachment, but she did not approach the colonel. In fact, at the sound of his voice, she moved behind the man who seemed most incensed by his commander's actions, as if shielding herself from more abuse.

The action had the desired effect. Gripping the man's arm from behind, she could feel him tensing, and saw that the soldier was staring hostilely at Bernhard.

The soldiers assembled, piled into the waiting vehicles, and drove off to the Sassi, leaving Marisa standing in the square.

Marisa sneered after the column of trucks. She was beginning to believe that her plan would succeed.

Chapter 37

One Day in the Sassi

The morning after his dinner with Arabella, Carlo ran into Martin again in the piazza where they decided to go to a café for breakfast. Over espresso and rolls, Martin proposed a tour of the area.

"I'm going back to the *Sassi* today, but without a guide. Would you like to join me?"

Carlo considered the idea. He had only visited the caves once, and he was curious about the civilization that existed there. He agreed, and Martin suggested meeting around ten o'clock.

They went in Martin's car, which he then parked in the same area where Santo had taken him the other day. As they mounted the steps leading to the first level of caves, Martin took out the journal. Inspecting the details on the pages in front of him, he looked up, then to the right, assessing his location from the words logged by Anselm so many years before. The caves were ancient and unchanged, so the descriptions offered by his grandfather two generations before were still valid.

"What's that?" asked Carlo, pointing to the journal.

Martin was a bit unsure how to answer. He had hidden the book and its origins from all the other people he had met because the Altamurans didn't trust him. On the other hand, this young American had treated him politely and seemed to be a reasonable person, so Martin decided to risk telling him the truth. Besides, he thought to himself, Carlo might already know so there was little to hide.

"It is my grandfather's journal, a book he kept of notes when he was in Italy during World War II." Referring to it merely as a war journal seemed less dangerous than revealing it as a treasure map.

"My grandfather was a German officer," he continued. Martin recited his well-practiced speech.

"He was sent into Italy to confiscate art for the Third Reich. What I can tell from this journal is that he kept some for himself." Martin's face assumed a certain pinkish hue, but he continued, "And it appears that he even abused some of the Italian people."

Martin's appearance in Altamura had resurfaced some of the villagers stories about the Nazis generally, and Colonel Bernhard specifically. Facts mixed with rumors, but stories were told in the cafés and on the street that linked Martin to the actions of the Germans so many years before. Carlo had heard some of the stories and so he knew that the abuse Martin spoke of was more specifically the abuse of women, but he let the words pass.

"This journal describes the art he found throughout Italy and who they belonged to. For the last few years I've tried to make amends for his thefts by seeking out the stolen materials and returning them to their rightful owners."

Now, Carlo pressed Martin for more information about the *Sassi*.

"What will you do if you find the treasure your grandfather was looking for here?"

Martin looked at his companion, but offered nothing in reply.

"Do you even know that it is here, in the caves?"

"All of his notes point to this, but, no, I don't know if this is where Anselm's fortune would be found."

Martin kicked at some rocks by his feet, inspected the journal once more with a cursory look, and pushed onward up the path with Carlo in tow.

Chapter 38

Down from the Hills

Anselm Bernhard descended the Murge and rejoined his troops by the trucks at the base of the plateau. Only Hilgendorf had gone up into the caves with him. The colonel didn't fear his men, but knew that if he found what he was looking for, he wouldn't want too many people to know about it.

But when he approached the troops milling about the trucks, he could tell that their mood had changed. He sensed an undercurrent of anger which he disregarded, knowing that German soldiers were conditioned to obey their commander, no matter what the circumstances. He counted on this training now.

Bernhard intended to find the hidden cache before the Allied advance reached Altamura, although reports from the front and the battle sounds all around reminded him of the danger he and his men faced. It also steeled his resolve, and hastened his search.

The convoy of trucks returned to Altamura and the colonel directed them to La Chiesa dello Spirito Santo. When his vehicle came to a stop, Bernhard jumped from the seat, strode up to the heavy wooden doors of the church, and rapped on them sharply with his wooden walking stick. The thudding reverberated off the stone walls throughout the interior of the church and, slowly, the doors creaked open.

The priest, Don Daniele, appeared in the doorway, squinting in the late afternoon sunshine. Bernhard told him to come out of the church and answer some questions, but when the priest exited the cool backdrop of the nave, Bernhard grabbed him roughly by the arm and pushed him into the truck waiting at the bottom of the steps.

The convoy then drove to the house that Bernhard had commandeered and he pushed the old priest through the door. In a moment, the woman who owned the house and who had been preparing the evening meal was pushed out of the same door, which slammed shut behind her.

His men then heard their colonel shouting questions in German and Italian, but little was heard from the priest. They also heard an occasional thud or whack, and other sounds of scuffling that went on for some time.

Soon, quiet came over the house, but then the questioning began again. In the meantime, a crowd had gathered outside. The German soldiers still stood by the front door, but the growing throng of villagers worried them. The troops wondered if they should retreat into the house – which Bernhard would not like – or disband and go back to their own quarters, away from this crowd.

The people outside heard shouted orders from within. The colonel's commands were clearly focused on the hidden wealth that he sought, and he accused the old priest of hiding information from him. He demanded to know where it was and how he could find it. His impatience was clearly amplified by his fear of the approaching Allies. Bernhard wanted to secure this great collection before he was forced to flee for his life.

Then there were sounds of whipping and breaking furniture, caught amidst the whimpering of the priest. After a few more moments, the house fell silent once again.

Yanking the front door open, Hilgendorf peered within. He heard the voice of his commander, so he entered. On the floor, bloodied from the beating, his head showing a gaping wound, the priest lay dead.

"Get him out of here!" Bernhard ordered.

Chapter 39

Dinner at Filomena's

Arabella joined Carlo and the family at Filomena's for dinner that night. Since she and Gia had been friends for so long her presence was not unusual, but both Zia and her daughter noticed that Arabella was especially pretty that night and wondered if Carlo's presence was responsible.

Cristiano also noticed the beautiful woman at the table, but from a careful distance since he saw that his adopted son was the focus of her attention. Everyone enjoyed a long and convivial meal, sharing platters of *pasta alla catalogna* – ziti cooked with chicory, then drained and dressed with garlic and tomato sauce, followed by *agostinelle* – floured and fried mullets served with lemon juice. All dishes enhanced by considerable quantities of Cristiano's wine.

About midway through the meal, the discussion turned to the German who was visiting Altamura. Carlo was careful not to repeat his earlier mistake of being too accepting of the outsider. His conversation with Arabella convinced him that the Italians, particularly those in the south, had not forgiven the Nazi regime for the terror they rained down on the villagers during the war.

During the conversation, Carlo looked for openings to defend Martin or at least to say charitable things about the young art collector. He made judicious use of these openings, but didn't press his case.

"The Germans nearly destroyed this town," Cristiano said through a mouthful of *Pane di Altamura*. "They tried, but we resisted, and we won."

"We survived," corrected Zia Filomena. "We wouldn't have won if the Americans hadn't come," giving Carlo a thankful nod of her head.

"The Nazis came to Basilicata, and stole from our families, our churches, and our shops, even though there wasn't much to steal," said Giovanna. "Everyone was poor, this wasn't a rich country, yet the Germans came and took whatever they wanted."

"Was there some military objective for them here?" asked Carlo.

"No. No military objective," Cristiano said. "But they knew we couldn't defend ourselves, so we were easy to rob."

"Some history books claim that the Germans wanted to control southern Italy so they could launch invasions of other places," Gia explained, "like North Africa, where they fought..."

"And lost," Cristiano said.

They were quiet for a few moments, and Carlo decided to raise Martin's name.

"But that young German fellow, he's not like the Nazis." And he was immediately sorry he tried to win that point.

"He's a bastard," blurted Cristiano. There was no room for debate, so Carlo dropped the subject.

Gia saw the anger in her father's face, so she changed the subject.

"Papa, Carlo was asking about Nino. I know a bit about his history, but not as much as you do."

"He's a gentle soul. His smile is not there, but he has grace in his heart," Cristiano began.

"Nino was born in sin, but he has worked in the convent and the church for... well, maybe seventy years. His whole life."

Emphasizing his point with his fork, he continued, "He is a saint."

Zia Filomena laughed. "He's not a saint. A simpleton maybe, and he has the Lord in his heart. But all he does is take care of the aging buildings. He can fix the pipes and electricity, and he can perform miracles with wood, but I don't think that makes him a saint."

"He's quiet," noticed Carlo.

"*Oh, sì*," said Zia. "As a mouse. Some people say he is following the vow of silence in memory of his mother, or of her sin. But I just think he has nothing to say."

Chapter 40

The German Retreat, September 11, 1943

A German battalion entered Matera in its march north ahead of the Allied onslaught. The Materani did not resist the initial occupation, but there was no longer any secret about Badoglio's surrender and the Italian cooperation with the American and British forces. So the occupation was tense, and produced some very predictable conflicts in the streets of Matera.

Outside the small town at the base of the Murge, and in the area surrounding nearby Altamura, the conflicts sometimes took the form of armed combat. The villagers used small arms to resist the Germans, who had more sophisticated weapons. With trained soldiers living among the residents of Matera and Altamura, these fights seldom went beyond guerrilla warfare, but both sides suffered casualties.

There was a lot of movement with the German columns, as detachments rumbled about readying for combat. The superior officers announced that their final objective was to move further north and form the Gustav Line, an east-west demarcation across the "ankle" of Italy's boot to dig in and prevent further encroachments by the Allies. The commander was Field Marshal Albert Kesselring, a highly decorated officer who had fought in the North African campaign and moved into Italy ahead of the Allied advance to stave off further losses.

He intended to set up a line of defense that the Allies couldn't break through, thereby saving northern Italy for the German regime.

The Altamurans knew that the German field marshal considered their region only as a battleground – a parched field between the Germans and the Allies that he would risk annihilating to further the cause of the Third Reich.

Chapter 41

Straniero

The next morning, as Carlo shared coffee and rolls in Filomena's kitchen, the talk returned to the young German visiting Altamura. It was obvious that neither Zia Filomena nor Cristiano trusted him. Their comments were openly disparaging, and any statements Carlo made that even slightly defended the man were waved away without a thought.

"The people of Altamura don't trust the German," Cristiano warned, and he told Carlo to avoid him.

"He's harmless," Carlo said, "and quite sincere in his quest."

"Stay away from the *straniero*," repeated Cristiano, thinking that calling Bernhard a foreigner would be enough to get his point across.

"But I'm a *straniero*, too," Carlo responded.

"No, you're not. You've got Italian blood in your veins."

"So did Mussolini," Carlo said.

"Mussolini was a Mexican," he snorted. It was common rumor that Mussolini's father gave him the name Benito after Benito Juárez, a Mexican radical in the 1800s. After *Il Duce's* fall from grace, the rumor provided Italians with a way to distance him from Italy and her heritage.

"You can't trust a Nazi," added Zia. "Look what they did to our town."

Gia burned with the same passion as her parents, but she let them carry the argument forward. Carlo listened, occasionally making a weak retort to restore order and fairness to the conversation, but he had no influence over his Altamuran hosts.

"Stay away from him," Cristiano said. And just as quickly, he rose from the table, threw his napkin down in disgust and left the room.

Chapter 42

September 12, 1943

With each day spent searching the Sassi, *the German soldiers became more concerned that dawdling in this dusty town would land them in POW camps. They could hear the sounds of distant battles and, despite German propaganda to the contrary, they knew that the Allies' cannons and aerial attacks were coming nearer.*

"But he's your commander," Marisa would say, and she sang empty praises about the man she was sleeping with in order to keep tabs on him. If she left him, or if he grew tired of her pleasures, her plan would not work. Marisa needed to stay close to him and maintain contact with the armed men who surrounded him.

There had been other nights when she considered reaching for the gun under Bernhard's pillow, but she hesitated. "I can't miss," she thought. "I may have only one chance and if I am not careful, he'll kill me like he killed Alessia." She was well aware of her sister's decision to take her own life that night in Venice, but Marisa still blamed the man that had used her and drove her to the action.

Marisa brooded often about Bernhard's role in her sister's fate, but didn't want to lose the opportunity for revenge by a hasty action. Besides, she still hoped to get help from the German soldiers who were growing disillusioned with their commander.

"He's going to have us killed," one soldier said to Hilgendorf. The lieutenant was becoming less willing to engage the conversation, knowing

that the troops were right and that his commander was making fatal mistakes in his obsessive search for a treasure that he wasn't even sure existed.

Just at that moment, Bernhard stepped out of the house and into the circle of soldiers. They parted to let him pass, except for one man who stood in his way. Stopping just inches from the younger man, the colonel stared into the man's face, a mixture of confidence and arrogance that revealed pride in his own position and dismissal of his men's interests. After a few seconds of this face-off, the soldier stepped to the side so that Bernhard could pass.

The colonel walked briskly by the man, brushing shoulders in a macho display of dominance.

Chapter 43

An Eye for an Eye

Getting even is a very human urge. Not revenge, per se. Revenge has overtones of reckless violence and sweeping destruction.

Getting even is more like just evening the score. The urge also carries the emotional reward of justice and fairness since the perpetrator is only applying the Biblical standard, an eye for an eye.

Marisa had fewer tools at her disposal to even the score for her sister's death. Bernhard was too powerful and the world was still at war.

She hoped to rely on the German soldiers under his command to provoke them to violence and to have them pay Bernhard back for her sister's death.

A simple pistol shot to the head would have satisfied Marisa, and she would have preferred to be the one pulling the trigger and watching the blood burst from the bastard's head.

But she worried that she would never get that close to him with a loaded weapon.

So she planned to turn the guns of the German army on him.

Chapter 44

Reworking the Journal

After spending the day with Carlo in the *Sassi*, Martin sat alone in his hotel room that night, turning pages in the journal and studying Anselm's cryptic messages under the dim electric light by his bed. A brighter light fixture was in the center of the ceiling in this modest room, but Martin decided not to use it since it would light up his window and he preferred the townspeople to know as little as possible about him – including what time he went to bed.

But his judgment was off because some low-level light still escaped through the curtains by his window, and it created an impression in the town that Martin was engaged in furtive activities within.

Outside the hotel, on the street below, two men observed the light. One pointed to Martin's room and whispered something; the second man blew out a column of smoke from his cigarette.

Further back from them, in the shadow thrown up by two adjacent buildings, another man watched with interest. His attention strayed occasionally to the men on the sidewalk as he concentrated on the dim light emitted from the window above.

Martin was oblivious to the surveillance and remained focused on the journal on his lap. He flipped back to the early pages, reading clear, concise passages about Italian churches, stolen art, and the women his grandfather had slept with. The narrative in the first half of the journal was straightforward and easy to understand.

Martin re-read these passages to familiarize himself with his grand-father's writing style, the better to piece together the odd notes and comments in the back of the journal devoted to the great secret in southern Italy.

He was more convinced than ever that this cache would be found in the area of Altamura or Matera, probably in the caves of the *Sassi*, and very likely in a church. He repeated the singular words that led him to this conclusion:

"*Kirche* – church," he said aloud, then looking about the darkened room, he lowered his voice. "*Wie der* Sassi – like the *Sassi*; meaning caves. *Im erdreich* – in the ground – made him think the caves would be underground, but there was still an incomplete picture in his mind. It was, however, the reason he spent additional time at the Chiesa di Santa Maria d'Idris in the caves.

Anselm had scribbled the word *kleister,* or was it *klotz*? The first meant paste; could it be a reference to the surface of the walls of the church? Was the art hidden behind the walls? *Klotz* meant block or stone, an easier connection but still not one that unlocked the secret.

Martin's mind wandered far afield. *Klotser* was an old slang terms for rings. Is it possible that there were rings in the church, perhaps near the altar, he thought? Or was Anselm simply dreaming about jeweled rings that he hoped to find?

Martin took out a pad and pen from his suitcase and began scribbling all the words he could think of to link the many separate phrases in his grandfather's journal. He kept the nouns and adjectives, added some verbs in varying forms, and continued juxtaposing the order to create sentences out of nonsense.

It was when he was applying this grammatical skill to the words that he struck upon an idea. He checked Anselm's notes, then checked his writing style in earlier passages to compare the letters as he wrote them. Just then, the scattered fragments of nouns and verbs changed suddenly into a new word, one that fit the phrasing. The word gleamed brilliantly in Martin's imagination; it nearly lifted off the page like a spirit.

Martin's muffled yelp of glee caught in his throat as a light thump sounded at his door.

Chapter 45

British Liberate Ferramonti, September 14, 1943

The Campo di Concentramento *at Ferramonti had functioned for over three years in Tarsia, a deserted landscape in Calabria, the toe of Italy's boot. It was the largest of Mussolini's camps for Jews and political dissidents, and it represented Il Duce's concession to Hitler that Italy would exercise a degree of anti-Semitism and detain the country's Jews.*

The first camp marshal was Gaetano Marrari, who viewed his responsibility as the protection of the human beings in his charge. No one was executed in Ferramonti; over the years only four internees died there, the result of Allied bombing, not the treatment of the camp's Italian guards.

The camp developed a reputation in the surrounding area as a place that also had prisoners from various professions. In fact, the medical care provided by some of the interned doctors was better than the people of Tarsia could get outside the camp since Italian country doctors were few and far between. With Marrari's cognizance, and with the guards' willingness to look the other way, it was not uncommon for someone from outside to sneak into the concentration camp to be treated by one of the doctors there.

When the lax security became known to passing German detachments, a Nazi general decided to pay a visit to the camp and evaluate it for himself. Sensing the threat to their autonomy, the camp chaplain raised a flag above the camp that suggested it was under quarantine. Then he ran to meet the general and warn him that cholera had hit the camp...but that he could enter at his own risk. The Nazi officer cancelled the visit and continued on his way.

But Ferramonti was still a concentration camp and it still held Italian political prisoners, foreign Jews, and even Catholics against their will. The Allies who were advancing had the concentration camp in their sights.

On September 14, 1943, British forces liberated Ferramonti and the internees were allowed to return to their lives on the outside...or what was left of such lives.

Chapter 46

Uprising in Matera

On September 21, 1943, two German soldiers assigned to a combat battalion entered a jewelry shop in Matera. Their intentions will never be known, but the shop owner suspected them of theft. By then, the Allies were marching up the boot and local villagers had grown bold enough to confront the remnants of German occupiers.

A bystander notified the local police of the suspected attempted robbery. In response, the police entered the shop catching the Germans still there. There was a confrontation and the two soldiers were killed.

This sparked an uprising, the boiling over of a simmering pot of hatred as the Materani took up arms against their oppressors. More German troops were killed by townsmen armed with pistols and carbines.

The Germans responded with force, using a cannon to blow up a building, and killing eleven Materani. But damage was limited because the Nazi commanders had already ordered the troops to pull out – the advance German forces for the Gustav Line were already fleeing north – so the soldiers in Matera left the insurrection behind, offering little retribution.

Chapter 47

Altamura, September 21, 1943

The detachment of German soldiers under Colonel Anselm Bernhard, however, remained in Altamura, although they had heard the news of the uprising in nearby Matera. They had long feared for their lives, and now they had ample reason to worry about the Italians possibly turning on them. Their commander's search for the treasure had become a burden that they no longer wanted to bear.

"What if he does find it?" asked one soldier. "Is he going to share it with us?"

Before anyone could answer, another man said, "I don't give a damn about the treasure. I want to get out of here before the Allies bomb us to hell."

"He's just digging around in the caves, the dirt, and the desert of this god-forsaken place," said the first. "There's nothing here. Bernhard's dragged us through this wasteland for – what? Nothing!"

Hilgendorf held up his hands to calm the tirade, but just as he was about to speak, a shot rang out.

The bullet came from behind him, lodging in the throat of the last man to speak, and blood spurted out of the gaping hole as the man grasped futilely at the mortal wound. The look of shock was drowned in brilliant red blood gushing from his neck, and a pained shriek escaped his lips before his body slumped to the ground.

Bernhard stepped into the circle of men, the muzzle of his pistol still smoking, and glared back at the mutinous soldiers around him. He would dress them down and remind them that there was a bullet for anyone who betrayed the Fatherland, but before he could begin his warning, another shot rang out from behind him.

A brass button on the colonel's jacket rocketed off his chest, pushed by the force of a bullet shot at close range from behind. Bernhard stood stock still for a second, watching the dark blood ooze from the hole in his chest, then turned slowly around, lifting his weapon to aim at whomever was standing there.

Marisa couldn't have gotten this close to the Nazi officer without his men's help. Or so she thought at first. But it was really Bernhard who had enabled her to stand before him at that moment, a gun raised to shoulder height. Without the colonel's selfish pursuit, he might have retained his soldiers' trust and protection.

But they had already decided that Bernhard was the traitor, and they stood motionless as the wounded but furious German officer raised his pistol to confront the woman who had slept in his bed.

Another shot rang out from Marisa's pistol and Bernhard's face erupted into fragments of bone and crimson blood, his arm caught only halfway to full height. Marisa had finally evened the score: for her sister, for all the other women he'd violated, and finally, for Italy.

Chapter 48

Sins of the Father

The maid tending Martin's room found his body the next morning.

As she had done every morning, on that day Analisa knocked at his door to make his bed and check the bath towel in the simple room that he occupied. Hearing no sound from within, she gently turned the handle and let herself in.

Martin was lying face down on the worn rug in the center of the room. His arms were splayed to the sides and his short hair was matted with coagulated blood. She screamed and ran from the room, down the steps and into the street as she called for a doctor, asking for help in the monstrosity that awaited in the hotel room above.

The sun was up and most of the people in Altamura were already about their business. Carlo was walking by the building when Analisa ran out into the light with a panicked look on her face. She grabbed him by the elbow, told him what had happened, then realized she was talking to another foreigner. As she ran past him to the piazza to get help Carlo slipped in through the open door of the hotel.

He entered Martin's room with some apprehension, having grasped the woman's plea, and looked down at the lifeless body of the young German whom he had befriended.

Martin's skull appeared crushed as if he was struck forcefully with a blunt object. Death probably came quickly, and Carlo made the sign of the cross as he stepped over the body.

After a cursory examination, he could tell that there was nothing he could do. Except for one thing.

Carlo remembered the journal, and Martin's secretive handling of it convinced Carlo that the journal contained information that was somehow the cause of Martin's death. He quickly examined the room but couldn't locate the book anywhere. Some of the bed was pulled apart, and the drawers to the dresser were open, so whoever did this to Martin was probably also looking for the journal.

Carlo sat on the edge of the bed and looked around the room.

"If the killer didn't find it," Carlo thought, "where would Martin have hidden the journal?"

At the sound of approaching footsteps from the stairwell, Carlo tensed up. He had to find the book before he was discovered there, or else he would have no other chance. He pushed aside the pillows, scattered Martin's clothing on the floor, lifted the rug and looked behind the curtains.

The footsteps became louder and closer.

Carlo pushed an art book off the nightstand to see what might be in the drawer. The book clattered to the floor and its leaves spread open. Martin's journal was pressed between some pages of the art book, pages that had been hollowed out to hold the journal.

Carlo lifted the journal quickly and shoved it into his pocket. He knew that Martin's presence in Altamura was not taken kindly by the villagers and in a moment of indecision, Carlo decided that the existence of the journal needed to be kept secret for a time, while he considered what its contents meant to his friend.

Carlo then closed the art book and returned it to the book shelf, thinking that the next person to search the room would find it but that would give him some time to make it to the street.

The police were too close to the hotel room door for Carlo to leave the building unnoticed. As the police watched, he stepped unsteadily out of the doorway as if hung over, covered his mouth as if he was going to vomit, and let them pass by.

Carlo stepped onto the sidewalk and looked around. There was the usual crowd, and he instinctively touched his pocket to ensure that the journal was still there. Then he turned down the street and onto another narrow avenue to escape the crowd.

The villagers ignored him, except for a tall man in the shadows across the street from the hotel where Martin's body was found.

Chapter 49

Piazza Veneto

In Altamura's Piazza Veneto that evening, the talk in all the cafés turned to Martin's murder, and his connection to Colonel Bernhard, then to the Germans back in the war. Carlo listened to the talk, and the whispered sidebars, and partly understood what the people of Altamura were feeling.

"He was another invader," said one man. "The Germans raped our village 70 years ago and, apparently, they weren't satisfied. So they sent this man." He waved his arm in a menacing gesture toward the window of the now-empty room where Martin had stayed.

Carlo, Gia, and Arabella met that night, departing from their customary *passeggiata* but not dropping from the conversation that captured everyone's attention that night.

"He probably deserved it," said Giovanna, but as soon as she said it, she regretted her words. They were harsh, but so were the Italians' feelings about the German invasion during the war, a memory still fresh.

Arabella recalled the civil uprising in Matera, triggered by the jewelry store that the German soldiers allegedly had tried to rob back in 1943. And she recounted other stories of homes and possessions confiscated by the Nazis, townspeople abused, animals slaughtered for the Germans' meals, and the women who were leered at – or worse – during the occupation.

"That's what they were like. The arrogance!" she nearly shouted. "They thought that they could take anything, anybody."

"But that was so long ago," said Carlo.

"That's the problem with you Americans. You say 'forgive and forget,' but it's not about forgiveness. It's about forgetness." Then she and Gia laughed a bit at the new word.

"You don't understand," Gia said to Carlo. "In America, you have too much." Arabella nodded her head, and Gia continued.

"In America, if something is old, you throw it away and get something new."

"And something better," chimed in Arabella.

Gia nodded assent, and continued. "You throw things away that are too old, even your parents and grandparents."

Carlo bristled at this, thinking that these women thought Americans were so cavalier as to discard their parents along with their possessions.

"We're not like that," said Arabella, picking up on Gia's theme. "Italians live in the past and the present at the same time. For us, nothing is old, nothing is new. It's all just there."

"What does that have to do with Martin's death?"

"It has to do with you, with Americans. In America, you have forgiven the Nazis, or at least forgotten them. We cannot."

Carlo knew that Americans lived with the horrible consequences of the Nazi campaign against innocents. He was proud that his countrymen had refused to let the immorality of the time fade from memory, but he had to admit that Europeans lived closer to the atrocities than did the Americans.

They were quiet for a while, as they crossed over one street and began another one. Then, to cool the emotions, Gia slipped her hand through Carlo's right arm, and Arabella slipped hers through his left.

They smiled awkwardly, each entertaining thoughts about their own country versus the other. And they recognized the differences between America and Italy, and how different interpretations of history and culture could alter the way they looked at the world.

They reached Arabella's house and she said, "And that is why I could never move to America," concluding the discussion for the night.

Chapter 50

A New Life

The Allied advance could be heard closing in on them, and the German soldiers wanted to retreat to safer areas north.

Hilgendorf stood over the bloody body of his colonel, regretting the man's death but pensive about what it meant for his own survival. In wartime, bodies were buried where they were slain, although it didn't seem that Bernhard's body would be moved by anyone now, certainly no one from this town that he had abused so egregiously.

The lieutenant didn't want to tarry long enough to do so himself. However, it was customary to return to the family of fallen soldiers some memento of their life, so he withdrew the journal from Bernhard's pocket and slipped into his own uniform. Looking around, and sensing the sound of gunfire getting closer, Hilgendorf departed quickly and worked his way out of the city. The detachment of soldiers had scattered, some in twos and threes, each focused on his own survival.

At the end of a street toward the outskirts of the town, he stopped and looked back. "What did we do?" he wondered. "What have we accomplished by invading this town, stealing its food and valuables, and leaving its people worse off? Are we savages?"

He turned on his heels when he saw Americans filtering through the streets of Altamura. Conscience was a guide, Hilgendorf thought, but only when the body survived to listen to it.

Marisa stayed behind as the German soldiers fled Altamura. In the moments after she sealed Bernhard's invitation to hell, she shook and cried, overcome by the realization of what she had done, relief that her sister's tragic death had been avenged.

She had nowhere to go, and her recent behavior painted her as a putana in the eyes of the villagers, so she doubted that she would be welcome to stay in Altamura. The war produced victims of all stripes; Marisa was a survivor who was bent on settling scores for her sister's death, and she had had to do objectionable things to accomplish this.

The people of Altamura could see more in her eyes than could the German officer she had taken up with. His culture was foreign and he couldn't read her; the locals knew that she was – like them – a tragic victim of the circumstances who was only doing what was necessary in very difficult circumstances. They could tell that her performance of late was a ruse – a dreadful, revengeful ruse – and they knew that this is what some of them had come to. That some of them would repeat, as Marisa had, behaviors that the Church would look upon with disgust, but which the Italian people would use if needed to avenge wrongs committed against their families.

After a day of searching for food, shelter, and a way to survive, Marisa was invited by a forgiving family to take meals with them. The next day, she was offered a job in a restaurant in town. It wasn't long before the first hopeful smile returned to her lips, and she thanked the people of Altamura for giving her new life.

Chapter 51

Don Adolfo in the Piazza

Even in his old age, Don Adolfo was a spirited man, a healer, a preacher and to the children of Altamura, their favorite playmate. Whenever he would pass through the town, he would greet people with a wave and a cheerful *"buon giorno,"* and if there were kids among the crowd, he would pay special attention to them.

Don Adolfo could easily step into a street game of soccer – or *calcio* – and his kick was as solid as the youngsters who egged him on. Threading between two defenders as much as his old legs would permit, he would hear children cheer and received their pats on the arm when he scored a goal.

Secretly, the old priest believed that the goaltenders who faced off with him were letting him score on kicks that were sometimes too soft.

Patting heads and chucking their chins after the short interlude on the pitch, Don Adolfo would leave the kids to play with a lightened spirit.

It was easy to see him as part of everyday life in Altamura, but hard to see him these days as the years began to pile up and his shoulders began to sag. There would still be youthful swings at the soccer ball, but he moved more slowly each afternoon as he walked away from the game.

One day, the holy *padre* seemed especially slow as he left the church. He stepped through the slightly opened wooden doors, and pull them closed with a practiced tug on the handle. But when he turned to face the sun and the steps leading down to the street, he winced at the light and held the rail of the steps tightly as he descended.

Don Adolfo shuffled down the street, mustering a smile to all he passed, but by the time he reached his residence, the nun at the door took him by the elbow and helped him inside.

At the door to his private quarters, the priest bade her goodbye and retreated to the familiar surroundings. The nun returned later that afternoon with a bit of food and drink, but when she saw the still body of her beloved pastor on the bed, she knew that he would not need anything on her tray anymore.

The nun hailed a passing villager and asked him to summon the other nuns. She told him that Don Adolfo was with the Lord, and that Nino would be required to help them prepare the priest for burial.

Over the next hour, a small crowd gathered outside the priest's house, peering into the open doorway and the window that the nuns had opened to allow the fresh air to enter, and Don Adolfo's spirit to leave. In that crowd, Carlo watched the women weeping. The men held their hats in their hands and wiped sweat – or was it tears – from their cheeks as they beheld their pastor one last time.

Nino had arrived by then and was handling Don Adolfo's body with care and love, his arms seeming to give the physical embrace that the other villagers could enjoy only spiritually.

Looking down on the old exhausted body, Nino spoke softly.

In both Italian and Latin, Nino said "Take the air and rise up, *mio padre*. The air is *per te*." Nino seemed oblivious to the crowd, and paid no attention to the fact that his words were overheard.

It is the first time Carlo heard Nino use the familiar "*te*" with the priest. It was then he realized that there was a connection between these two men.

Chapter 52

La Chiesa dello Spirito Santo

Carlo tugged at the metal handles of the church door, drawing it open just enough to slip inside. It was mid-morning and most of the early prayers had been said, and the parishioners had departed.

He wanted to savor the deep quiet of the stone structure. The cool air welcomed him, the dim light cast by the candles on the altar lured him into a contented hypnotic state, and the stillness of the air rewarded him with a nonintrusive, uninterrupted peace.

He walked with soft footsteps down the stone aisle toward the altar, rested his hand on the endpost of the second pew, and settled into a seat there.

He looked up at the crucifix and realized that it was made in the same image as the one in St. Ambrose Church in St. Louis. Carlo turned his head left, then right, and smiled at the concordance of the Stations of the Cross. Even the holy water font reminded him of his home.

Carlo made the sign of the cross and folded his hands in his lap. He didn't pray as much as he reminisced about the people of Altamura and its region, Basilicata, and the hundreds of generations of Italians who had lived in the *Sassi*.

He thought about Martin, and his sudden violent death. About Don Adolfo, the kindly old man God had allowed to live a peaceful life into old age. He thought about the war stories he had heard of the Germans, and how the people of this gentle town persevered through war, famine, and hard times but could still participate in the evening *passeggiata* and enjoy the company of three or four generations gathered around the dinner table.

Carlo thought about Italian culture. He had come to Altamura to discover his roots, thinking that it was the dinner table, the food they shared, or the wine that they drank with gusto. In the end, he realized that Italian culture was about love and survival, about turning to, and shoring up the family you were born into. It was about sharing the secrets and the traditions, from trivial daily rituals to sacred religious ceremonies. And sometimes it was about revenge.

Italian culture was about the family, about the people, and about the bonds that held them together.

He remained there, in silent prayer, for some time, so long that he didn't notice that Nino had appeared at the altar. The old man collected some prayer books left by the kneeler, checked the linens on the altar stone, and then turned to leave before noticing that there was a penitent sitting in pew number two.

Nino stepped down from the altar and approached Carlo, but just then the outer door of the church swung open. Giovanna appeared in the sunlit opening; Nino looked up at her, and then decided not to approach Carlo. He stepped lightly past pew number two, reached the back of the nave, and nodded to Gia as he exited the church through the main doors.

Giovanna strode up the main aisle and rested her hand lightly on Carlo's arm. He was surprised that the old man didn't stop to talk to him. At Gia's touch, Carlo rose to escort her from the church.

Chapter 53

Return to Berlin

Hilgendorf worked his way north over the coming weeks. First through the region of Lazio and its city, Rome. Up through Liguria, then the Piedmont region, finally into Switzerland and from there to Germany.

The men in the detachment had long since gone their own ways. He knew that was the way of things, and he also knew that moving along a route separately was the safest way for each of them to escape the advancing Allied forces.

In mid-October, he reached Berlin. He discreetly asked for information about Colonel Anselm Bernhard's wife – his widow. Hilgendorf knew that the German army was desperate for soldiers and he would get redeployed easily if his identity became known, or if the forces gathered around Berlin realized that he was retreating from the campaign in southern Italy.

So the young lieutenant kept to himself as much as he could. After a few careful inquiries, he was able to find where Frau Bernhard lived.

He walked up the steps to her second floor apartment and rapped lightly on the door.

The sight of a soldier at the door, with hat in hand, was never welcomed by any family in times of war. Frau Bernhard's reception was wary, at best. After some brief introductions, she invited Hilgendorf inside.

In the older woman's living room, the young officer reported that her husband had died a hero's death at the hands of the enemy. He confined his description of affairs to modest activities that Frau Bernhard would neither understand nor challenge, and he left soon after the conversation began.

Hilgendorf kept the existence of the journal secret until their meeting was nearly over. He knew that the contents would be disturbing to Frau Bernhard, and he preferred to be heading back down the flight of steps and exiting the building before she had a chance to read its contents.

Chapter 54

Café Romano, in Altamura

Carlo sat in the shade of an umbrella outside Café Romano, drumming his fingers on the table. A half litre of the local red wine stood on the table alongside a shallow bowl of nuts and olives. He sipped the wine and absentmindedly chomped on an almond, but his thoughts were on the notebook in his pocket, and the sound of Nino's voice on the phone earlier that day.

The caretaker had wanted to meet with him, said it was urgent, but Carlo knew that the urgency stemmed solely from Nino's demanding the meeting. Still, Carlo decided to honor the request, and found himself in the piazza, under this umbrella, in the heat of the afternoon.

Just as he took another sip of wine, he saw Nino crossing the square at a deliberate, yet unhurried, gait. He made a bee line to Carlo's table, sat down across from him without any social pleasantries, and locked eyes with Carlo.

"You have it," Nino said, more of a declaration than a question.

"Yes, I do," replied Carlo. He didn't want to become part of a scene he couldn't control. He didn't even want to be in Altamura since Martin Bernhard's murder. Carlo wanted to remind Nino that he was only a visitor, only here to learn more about Italian culture. He didn't want to know anything about the murder or, for that matter, anything about Altamura's secrets. At that moment, he only wanted to be back home, but he kept such thoughts to himself.

Carlo didn't want to give the notebook to Nino. He wasn't sure why the caretaker wanted it, or how he knew of its existence, but Carlo felt that somehow this notebook was the cause of Martin's death and he didn't want it destroyed.

"You will give it to me," Nino said flatly.

"Why?"

Nino gave Carlo a menacing stare – and then...

"Follow me," he said. They walked across the piazza, and passed through a door on the side of the church. Leaving the bright sunshine and entering the dimly lit Chiesa dello Spirito Santo made it hard for Carlo to see at first, and the darkness and cool air of the apse made him even more apprehensive.

Nino walked past the rows of pews and pushed open a door at the other side of the altar. He stopped and, looking over his shoulder, jerked his head signaling Carlo to follow.

The two men entered a small room that smelled of incense and was lit by a single stained glass lamp suspended from a long chain from the middle of the vaulted stone ceiling.

Nino drew up two chairs, positioned them along one wall, and sat down. He pointed to the other as his eyes locked with Carlo's, who settled into the other hard wooden chair. Their knees were almost touching and Nino's large frame seemed to loom over Carlo. Yet the younger man was not afraid. The drama, menace, and isolated meeting place didn't alarm him. Instead, Carlo felt he was about to learn more about the notebook and Altamura's secret.

Nino leaned forward, sighed, and began to speak.

Chapter 55

La Chiesa dello Spirito Santo

"Altamura is a small village, not one that most American tourists come to see," Nino began.

"But we are a proud people, and we are blessed by the grace of the *La Chiesa dello Spirito Santo*. Our town is known to many Italians as a holy city, and there are stories of saints who have caused miracles to happen here. So, even without American tourists, we have many pilgrims visiting Altamura each year to pray in our church and take water from our fountain."

Carlo knew this and even met some of the *paisani* who came to the village to kneel and pray in the church, thus paying their respects to the saints of ancient times.

"This has been known for many years – centuries," Nino continued, "which is why – when the Germans invaded our land – the priests, nuns, and townspeople came to Altamura with their most precious possessions to hide them from the wartime pillaging."

"What did they bring" Carlo asked, "and where did you keep it?"

Nino ignored Carlo's questions.

"It took weeks, maybe months," he continued, but the villagers kept coming. Our pastor during the war, Don Daniele, welcomed them all. He blessed them as they arrived, tenderly took their possessions, and blessed the people as they left the church."

Nino paused as thoughts of his mother passed through his mind, reminding him how the war had affected the gentle people of Italy.

"By the time the Germans arrived, all these things were safe."

Carlo didn't want to pause Nino in his story, but his curiosity about the possessions and their whereabouts nearly overcame his patience.

"But there was this one officer, Colonel Anselm Bernhard." As Nino he uttered the name, he looked meaningfully at Carlo, convinced that the colonel was related to the young German curator who had recently 'invaded' his town.

"Bernhard the bastard," Nino said. "That's what we called him, behind his back of course. He was a ruthless man who violated our women and ransacked the town. He said he knew we were hiding something but since he couldn't find it he would leave Altamura scarred forever. Don Daniele was a proud man, and stood toe-to-toe with Bernhard, his chin jutting out defiantly, so the bastard knew the priest was keeping a secret.

"Bernhard hit the old priest with his riding crop, right across the face. They were standing on the steps of the Chiesa dello Spirito Santo and the people were crying and praying for mercy for their blessed pastor. But Bernhard, unmoved, smiled and struck him again.

"Don Daniele never gave in, so the Germans took him away. For hours we could hear his cries. Bernhard tortured our priest in a lockup that would be the last thing that the holy Don Daniele would ever see.

"The bastard and his troops stayed in Altamura for a while longer but then moved on, probably to torture and pillage another Italian town. When the bishop heard of what had happened, he came here to bless and console us, and to announce that he had chosen a new pastor, Don Adolfo, who lived in this village ever since, until passing away just recently. But you already knew that," Nino added, and he paused for a moment's reflection, before revealing another of the town's secrets.

Chapter 56

A Blunt Object

"Don Adolfo was my father," Nino admitted.

"He committed a sin with my mother during the panic of the war. He had already taken his vows and was a priest, so it was a great sin before God. The bishop knew and wanted to punish him, and he decided that Don Daniele's death was a perfect opportunity for penance. The bishop assigned my father to Altamura, where he would be near my mother, near me, and live every day knowing what he had done. We hardly ever spoke, and he believed he kept his secret from me all these years, but I knew.

"My mother lived out her life in the convent. She never took the vows or wore the habit of a nun. She said her sin made her unworthy. But she made her place in a small storeroom where I lived for the first few years of my life, until it was unseemly for a young boy to be sleeping in his mother's room. So I moved in with the Cantones and grew up there, but like my mother I continued to work at the convent and church, doing small jobs and helping to repair things as I could.

"What happened to your mother?" Carlo asked.

"She was lonely every day of her life. She seldom smiled, and seemed to bear the weight of her sin in every waking moment."

Nino looked down and grew quiet, pained to recall those difficult years.

"She helped protect the things that were entrusted to us, to the *Chiesa dello Spirito Santo*, keeping them secret until the rightful owners returned to claim them. Some did, some died in the war, but my mother never gave up her sacred trust to protect the possessions that had been delivered to the church. And mixed among the personal possessions were other things too precious to risk. So if they must remain hidden, it was through her efforts that these precious items would remain safe. When she passed away some years ago, I took on the responsibility, with the prayerful support of Don Adolfo."

"And they're still here, still hidden?" Carlo asked.

This question shook Nino out of his reminiscences.

"Yes, and they would have remained safe if the Germans hadn't sent another one down here with that damned notebook to ferret out the secret."

"But the notebook doesn't mention Altamura," Carlo protested, "and it doesn't even seem to identify the things Anselm was looking for, except to say that some small town in southern Italy houses a great fortune, a town with an old church named after a great spirit. But all saints are spirits. And Martin Bernhard wasn't sent here by the German government."

Nino shook his head in disagreement. Distrust of Germans was deep-seated throughout southern Italy, the first regions to abandon Hitler, Mussolini, and the Axis powers and side with the Allies during the war.

"If you trust the Germans, you're stupid. The people of Altamura never will, and I pray that the rest of Italy remains firm in this also."

Carlo had come to know and like Martin, and believed that the young curator's intentions were good, but he also knew that arguing this point with Nino would be useless. Anselm Bernhard's wartime notebook included both reverential descriptions of Italian art and despicable anecdotes of the sexual practices that the author had forced upon the Italian girls. Martin had annotated many of the entries, using red ink to distinguish his additions and to identify artworks that he had recovered and returned to the people or churches from whence they had been stolen. Many of the passages were so noted, Carlo recalled, but there was only one red mark in the special section at the back, the section that more and more seemed to him to be a coded reference to Altamura. That mark was *kloster.*

"After Don Daniele accepted the personal belongings from the surrounding villages," Nino continued, "he stored them away for safekeeping. He entrusted only my mother with this secret. When he died, my mother was afraid that the secret would die with her. In one of the very few conversations that ever took place between my father and mother, she told him of the things taken in by Don Daniele and where they were hidden. Then, at her death, the responsibility passed to Don Adolfo, where it has remained for all these years."

"You sound as if you know where these things are hidden," Carlo suggested.

"Just before she died, my mother entrusted the secret to me. She was afraid that some terrible thing might happen to my father before the knowledge was relayed to someone. For a while, three people knew of the great things and where they were hidden; after her death, the secret returned to just two trusted souls."

"But Don Adolfo is gone, so now it's only one," Carlo said.

"Yes, me, but the secret is also known to anyone who possesses that notebook," Nino added, pointing to the bulge in Carlo's pocket.

"I've read the journal," Carlo said, "especially the last part. I don't think it points directly to the *Chiesa dello Spirito Santo,* or even to Altamura."

Nino was unconvinced. He extended his right hand but Carlo wasn't ready to hand over the journal.

"What if these precious things rightfully belong to other churches and villages in Italy?" Carlo asked.

Nino was unmoved by the question. He knew the importance of the treasure in Altamura, and he wouldn't be persuaded by Carlo to compromise it.

"Dello Spirito," was all he said at first, then he added, "The Spirit. Altamura is a very poor village, and these things are not anything in an earthly sense, but they are the spirit that raises us up. We will never surrender them."

This was said with such finality that Carlo realized that there was no point in carrying the debate further.

Extending his right hand once again, Nino simply said, "The book."

Carlo watched Nino's right hand reach toward him as his left hand reached for a long-handled shovel next to him.

The book or a crushed skull.

Carlo had no choice.

He handed the journal over to Nino and walked out of the room.

Chapter 57

Hidden Treasures

Nino took the journal, walked out of the church, and went to the convent. He entered the storeroom that served as his mother's living quarters during her many years of penance among the nuns. As he thumbed through the journal out of curiosity, and saw the red-inked additions made by Martin in the final chapters of the book.

Kloster. Nino couldn't speak German, but he could tell the word sounded a lot like cloister, or convent. Perhaps the young German had uncovered the secret after all.

He gently lifted the few boxes that stood upon the wooden mantle of his mother's former bed. When she lived there, her quarters were spare, a wooden plank nailed down to a short stone riser served as her bed, upon which she allowed only a thin straw mattress for sleeping.

Nino pried up several of the nails holding the palette in place, nails that emitted a slight wail as they were withdrawn from their long resting place. Once freed from their pinioned position, the iron stilettos fell to his feet, and Nino folded back the palette itself. With the journal in one hand and a lantern in the other, he stepped down into the well that opened before him.

It was a cavern that had existed for years before his mother took up residence in the supply room. It served the convent as a root cellar and wine cellar in the past, and had been forgotten by the cloister over time. But the space was resurrected to a new use by Sofina.

"I want you to store these precious objects from the churches of the region down there," Don Daniele had told her. "There they will be safe from the Germans."

"But what if someone discovers it?"

"No one will," he said. "Not even the sisters of this convent know that the cellar exists. It was last used over thirty years ago, before any of the new novitiates, and before the Mother Superior arrived in Altamura."

Sofina was ready to obey, but wondered how the priest himself knew of the cavernous hole. As if reading her mind, Don Daniele smiled and addressed her.

"I have been here for many years, Sofina. When you pull back the palette that you use as a bed and you peer into the darkness, you may find some empty wine bottles still keeping a vigil over the place."

Nino thought of this part of the story his mother had passed on to him, and he allowed a slight smile to adorn his wrinkled face. So old Don Daniele imbibed a bit more than altar wine; so what.

From her own telling, Nino knew that his mother had scraped the walls of the cellar to smooth the surfaces, then carried the dirt out in buckets, keeping her actions as unnoticed as possible to protect the secret that lay within. Sofina had smelled the rich earth below the floor and knew that it was fertile soil, so she came upon an idea of how to dispose of the dirt that she would extract from there.

Working slowly, a pail at a time, she extracted the scrapings and small piles of long unused soil from their subterranean confines, fitting the room out for its new, more important role. In the early morning air, she would carry the pails of dirt outside the convent walls to fertilize her garden. Pride is a sin, she reminded herself often, but she couldn't help feeling a bit of pride for the beautiful flowers and vegetables that the garden offered up. The nuns who toiled around her were jealous – another sin – but they had to agree that Sofina grew the most amazing things under God's sun.

At night, Sofina prayed that the soil was not only fecund, but blessed to come from consecrated earth. It was in this cavernous space, below her palette, inside this convent, that Sofina hid the true treasures of the Italian churches scattered about the region – the relics of bygone centuries that had been carried by the faithful during the war years to be stored for safekeeping in the care of the church.

There were desiccated fingers of saints, whisps of hair from holy men, bone fragments that were believed to have come from Christ's apostles, even splinters from the original Cross. There was no gold, no jewels; instead this crypt held things far more dear to the Italians than worldly goods: the physical remains of the saints and the earliest years of Christianity.

Nino placed the journal on a shelf, bowed his head and made the sign of the cross, then turned to a darkened corner of the hollow space and fixed the lantern light on a small indentation in the clay subsoil that made up the wall of this space.

Chapter 58

The Papyrus

Nino gently dug the clay padding around the indentation and opened up a small space behind the wall. From it he extracted an ancient stone box and lifted the lid to reveal an old, yellowed cloth wrapped loosely around another object.

Nino gently withdrew the cloth, revealing a scattered stack of papyrus fragments. The text on the antique scraps was unfamiliar to him, written in the ancient Coptic language common during the time of Christ. Nino knew that he couldn't translate it, but he recalled his mother's recitation of the heading: "This is the Gospel of Matthias, as passed down to his son Gaius, and then to Gaius' sons, Jacob and Aramus."

In the dusty plains of Palestine, a holy man walked behind his Lord, a man of saintly heritage that many people said was sent by Yahweh, the god of the Jews. The holy man, Matthias, was not yet chosen to be among the small band of disciples, but he was warmed by the grace and smile of his Master. Matthias followed him on his daily rounds, listened intently to his words, and memorized the lessons the saintly leader left with the believers who flocked to hear him speak.

Through instructions from her priest, Sofina had come to understand some of the words on the scroll, but only enough of the ancient language to appreciate what she – now he – held in their hands.

Repeating his mother's words rather than translating them himself, Nino said, "This is the true Gospel of Matthias, a disciple of Jesus, who walked with Him for many years, and who was adopted as an apostle by Jesus' closest followers after His death."

When their Lord was taken prisoner and then crucified, many of the disciples fled, fearing for their lives. Judas was called out as the traitor, but he hanged himself from a barren tree on the plains around Jerusalem. Even Peter, the leader of the disciples, denied the Lord three times when questioned by the soldiers.

It was an ancient text from the first century of Christianity, written by Matthias just a few years after Jesus lived, decades earlier than the other gospels, by someone who knew Jesus intimately while He was still on earth.

Matthias remained true to his Lord, escaping the grasp of the authorities and refusing to deny the divine promise of the sainted man. He had been a prophet and the gentle people of this land had waited many years for His coming, and Matthias was not going to be the one to turn on Him.

Matthias had followed Jesus through the fields, villages, and cities. "He heard His speeches firsthand," Sofina had told Nino, "and watched the glow of redemption come over the faces of the people He addressed." Matthias had firsthand knowledge of Jesus' meaning and His intent, so he was the natural choice of the apostles to join their band and spread the teachings throughout the region and the world following the crucifixion.

When the disciples emerged from hiding, they decided to carry on the teachings of their Lord. And Matthias, the most steadfast among them, was allowed to join them in their crusade. He was the most educated of the disciples and persisted in taking notes of the Lord's teachings and the sermons that he gave throughout Palestine. It was by Matthias's hand that the disciples expected to chronicle the life of this holiest of men, the prophet who had brought them hope.

This text, the words revealed on the papyrus in Nino's hands, recounted the experiences and teachings of Jesus while he was still alive, spoken in the exact words of Matthias, as passed down to his grandson Jacob who wrote the words upon this sheet. Nino had asked his mother about the papyrus, and she told him that there have been legends about the lost Gospel of Matthias for many centuries, but few scholars believed that it actually existed.

This was that gospel, but translated in the hand of Matthias' grandson, and it had been lost for nearly two thousand years until an unknown pilgrim brought it to Altamura during the war. Don Daniele had asked where it came from, but the dark-skinned and hooded pilgrim was terse.

"Keep it safe, padre," the pilgrim whispered. He looked only once into the priest's eyes, then turned and vanished into the crowd.

Matthias was zealous about his responsibility. He wrote down as much as he could of his Lord's words and parables, and rendered this into a long narrative of the life that had rescued true believers from darkness.

Nino remembered his mother's fervent recitation of the passages that she could recall from the priest's teaching. How the words of Matthias told of lives and truths that Jesus meant when He still spoke as a man, as the living Son of God, before His death and resurrection. It was Matthias, through his grandson Jacob's careful copying, that the true, direct words of Jesus could be read.

Nino knew all this only from his mother's telling, since he couldn't translate the words himself. Holding the fragments of papyrus gently in his big hands, Nino wept. He knew that this possession was worth more than any relic on earth, but that he could not let anyone know about it. He also knew from the translated passages that the sainted man, called Lord by Matthias, was not the son of God as many have claimed since that time. To expose the existence of the Gospel of Matthias would be to deny the divinity of Jesus and probably lead to the destruction of the parchment.

After pausing in reverence, Nino refolded the fragments into the protecting cloth and thence into the stone box, and lifted it carefully back into its resting place in the earthen wall of this cavern. Then he carefully repacked the earth around it, and climbed the ladder back out of the space.

Chapter 59

Staying True to Altamura

The people of Altamura saved Marisa's life, in more than simply physical ways. They took her in after she shot Anselm Bernhard, hid her from the ragtag remnants of German soldiers straggling back from the battlefields who would have taken her into custody. They even hid her from the Americans to avoid complications and questions that might have made Marisa's life more difficult.

Hiding a Venetian woman in the Mezzogiorno shouldn't have been so easy. Northerners have a lighter complexion and, if that didn't give her away, her dialect would have. There is very little correspondence between the Italian language spoken in Venice and that spoken in the south, but the Allied soldiers didn't know that.

So Marisa blended in and made her home in Altamura. When the war was winding down and some of the Italian soldiers were returning to their hometowns, a young sergeant named Guido Valcone came back to Altamura. His body was broken in ways that would never heal, and his spirit had been shaken, but standing in the shadow of the Chiesa dello Spirito Santo lifted him up.

"My broken arm will still serve me well, and this limp is just a reminder of our sacrifice," he said. "But my heart and soul belong here."

Soon, the people of Altamura put Marisa and Guido Valcone together, sensing that both of them needed someone, and that pairing those shaken by war tragedies was God's plan.

Marisa married Guido not long afterward and bore three children who were healthy and happy in this tiny town in the Mezzogiorno.

Guido told his children about the war, about the suffering, and about his trials at the front. But Marisa would never share any of her experiences with them. She remained ashamed of how she had cornered Anselm Bernhard, but fiercely proud that she had avenged her sister, Alessia.

The Valcone family grew up in Altamura, as Guido and Marisa worked with the villagers to rebuild the war torn region.

Chapter 60

So Soon, Too Soon

"You're leaving," said Arabella. It was a question but sounded more like a certainty.

"Yes," replied Carlo, "to St. Louis."

"What's the name of your saint, the church you attend in St. Louis?"

"Saint Ambrose."

"Well," Arabella said with some resolve, fighting back the tears. "I will pray to Sant' Ambrose to keep you well."

She tried to stay resolute, but couldn't help adding, "and that he might bring you back to me one day."

They looked at each other with both love and sympathy. Carlo knew that he would not be returning, at least not to live there. Altamura was a wonderful town and he had come to know more about his Italianism in this village, including the vast difference between being an Italian and being an Italian-American. But that epiphany was telling him to go home, to be with his family, to carry on the culture and traditions of Italy, to cherish his parents, aunts, uncles, and cousins. And the siblings that he missed so much.

Like Arabella, he had grown up in a culture where food, wine, and big family gatherings were the norm. With aunts pinching cheeks and uncles wrapping the kids in bear hugs, there was always music, laughter, and tight family connections.

Some traditions were taken directly from the old country, especially the food that was closely reminiscent of southern Italy's best. Carlo had even helped some Italian neighbors on The Hill in St. Louis stomp the grapes and make wine in just the manner that Cristiano did in Altamura. Now, with more knowledge of breadbaking rituals, he knew that he could turn out loaves to match those of Zia Filomena – if he only could find a stone oven.

But not every Italian tradition survived in America.

He looked at Arabella again, imagining having children with her, but although they honored similar traditions, they came from different worlds.

With tears staining her cheeks, Arabella stood resolutely before Carlo. She was fighting against giving in to sadness or longing, but he was willing to cross the space between them.

Taking Arabella in his arms, Carlo kissed her and whispered in her ear.

Chapter 61

Too Long, Too Lonely

Carlo left Arabella that day and he shared a loving goodbye meal with his host family that evening.

He left Altamura the next day. He would never know what became of Arabella, if she ever married or had children. But he thought of her often.

He drove his rental car back to Bari, turned it in, and boarded a train for Rome. The hours rolled by as the train rumbled across the land, passing from the arid reaches of the Mezzogiorno to the more fertile landscape of central Italy.

Carlo arrived in Rome on the day before his flight back to the United States. He stayed at the same hotel he had used weeks before, and wandered off into the afternoon sunshine as he had done that day upon arriving in the Eternal City.

It's true what Arabella and Gia said about Americans, Carlo thought. "We have so much, it's easy to wave off the experiences of the past." The southern Italians, the people who lived on land that had been invaded and occupied by so many cultures over the centuries, could not as easily dismiss those events as worthy only of the history books. They still lived them today.

Was that good, he wondered? If the people of Altamura had more of what the Americans enjoyed, would they turn away from re-living the past and live in the present? Would that even be the best thing?

Carlo walked past monuments and fountains in the streets of Rome that had stood for centuries. The faces on the sculpted monoliths looked just like the faces of the people sitting at the cafés. The ruins of the city center, including the Forum, had not been paved over for a high-rise office building. These ruins stood there because they were still there. Because Romans – and Italians – don't discard the past or pretend it didn't happen.

He sat down at a café and ordered a Campari and soda. The rustic wines of the south were appropriate in the simple life in the Mezzogiorno, but it seemed like this little cocktail, one that Carlo had come to appreciate as an adult, was more in place in the urban atmosphere of this great city.

But wine or Campari, the Italian people would always be who they are, and the Americans would always be who they are. He looked down into the glass and shook it to make the ice cubes rattle around, and he thought of Arabella.

He missed her, as he missed all of the Filomena family and the people of Altamura, but he knew in that moment that he could not have made her happy in St. Louis. And she could not have made him happy in her village.

Chapter 62

Passing on the Burden

Nino slumped on the edge of his bed, hands folded in his lap, his face showing the weariness of age and the burden he now carried alone. His mother had died many years ago, and now his father, Don Adolfo, was gone too.

The secret of Altamura was hidden deep underground, in a cellar that everyone had long since forgotten – a secret of such immense importance that it seemed to Nino to have become nearly alive in its own right. He stared down at his wrinkled hands, unmoving, and considered what his next steps should be.

"Protect the secret always," Don Adolfo had told him. "Protect not only the relics and the papyrus, but also the knowledge of where they are kept."

Nino had eliminated the German art collector, then retrieved the journal from the American, so outsiders could not find the gospel. In his silence among the townspeople, he knew that others had not found out and would probably never know. He considered that to be his mission – keep the cavern safe from intruders.

But Nino couldn't shake an uncomfortable feeling. He knew that, by doing nothing, the secret would die with him, a prospect that in these later years of life he knew was not too distant.

Rising slowly, he walked toward a small desk in the corner of his room and sat down heavily into the chair. Taking up a paper and pen, he wrote a brief note, using vague terms and in language that would be understood by only person. Holding the paper up before his eyes to inspect it and, questioning his motives and the correctness of his decision, he laid it down on the desk for a moment.

Reading his words once more, he signed it, folded it neatly, and inserted it into an envelope that he had taken from the drawer. Licking the gummed edges and applying light pressure to seal the envelope, Nino turned the package over and picked up the pen. On the envelope, he wrote:

Carlo DeVito

St. Louis, Missouri

United States of America

Then he slipped the sealed envelope into the drawer of the nightstand next to his bed.

Chapter 63

One Last Visit

Arabella sat in her chair staring out into the sunlit piazza beyond her house. She wondered what Carlo was doing, if he had made it safely back to Rome, and whether he had already boarded the airplane for the States.

Then she stood and walked directly out the door. Thoughts of Carlo and what had transpired in Altamura in recent days made her think more about her family, and about what they had experienced. She had not visited her parents for a few days, since spending time with Carlo, and she wanted to stop by for dinner at their house.

But before going there, she had a mission to complete.

She bought a bunch of flowers at the local market and drove a short distance out of town. Before seeing her mother, she wanted to visit her grandmother, and she would appreciate the flowers.

Turning south down the lane and taking only a few minutes to arrive at her destination, Arabella stopped the car just inside the gates of the cemetery. It was only a little hill up to the site of her grandmother's grave, and Arabella took the climb with ease.

She stopped at the foot of the grave and lay the flowers on the green grass, then made the sign of the cross. When she had finished her brief prayer, she laid her hand on the gravestone, and traced her fingers across the name etched there.

"Marisa Valcone," she said aloud, "beloved wife and mother." That and the date was all that appeared on the stone, but Arabella knew that her grandmother's life meant so much more to her and to the rest of the family.

"A man travels the world in search of what he needs,
then he returns home to find it."
George Augustus Moore
Irish poet

Afterword

Altamura and Matera are real towns in southern Italy, just as the Sassi really exist, and just as the Nazi crimes described here were really committed against the Italian people.

So, too, did the great treasure exist, and Matthias, and his memories – all now lost to the ages.

Perhaps it is buried somewhere in the southern regions of Italy, where so many of the people of the early Christian church ended up; perhaps it is hidden somewhere in a very private collection in Germany, hidden from public view to protect the stories that the Church wishes to be kept from view.

And, perhaps, it will one day be found.

Acknowledgements

In the course of researching and writing a book, the author is pictured as a lonely laborer, pouring through odd books and dog-eared journals in the dark hours of the night to capture the details of a plot then pecking away at a keyboard to arrange the words in artful fashion.

There were many nights spent just this way but, in truth, the author labors at the writing desk in the shadow of all those who have supported him and advised him throughout the process of creation. I could not have gotten through this without my wife, Linda, my toughest critic but also my most durable source of insight and inspiration; or without the love and encouragement of my daughter, Kristen, who always makes me feel like a success before I've even begun the task.

Editing can be a trying and tedious business, but at the hands of my good friend and tireless editor, Dona deSanctis, it became a motivating influence. Dona didn't miss a mistake, that's true, but her greatest contribution to this work was not catching what I did wrong but reminding me of what I needed to do right. More help with ideas and staging came from Holly Harrington. Good friends and supportive family members, including Laura Lake, Don Rosano, and Mike Hutsell formed a core of early readers, whose thoughts and suggestions probably saved Dona from finding even more errors in her professional review.

I have long been led by the example of other Italian and Italian-American writers. Principle among them is Paul Paolicelli, an accomplished author himself and a source of endless ideas. And I must thank

Robert M. Edsel and Bret Witter, authors of *Monuments Men*, upon whose book I wrote a chapter in mine.

Thanks to all for the help, advice, support, and belief in my writing.

Dear reader,

We hope you enjoyed reading *The Secret of Altamura*. Please take a moment to leave a review, even if it's a short one. Your opinion is important to us.

Discover more books by Dick Rosano at
https://www.nextchapter.pub/authors/author-dick-rosano

Want to know when one of our books is free or discounted? Join the newsletter at http://eepurl.com/bqqB3H

Best regards,
Dick Rosano and the Next Chapter Team

About the Author

Dick Rosano is a wine, food, and travel writer with long-running columns in *The Washington Post, Wine News, Wine Enthusiast* and other magazines. He has five recent books on wine. *Wine Heritage: The Story of Italian-American Vintners* chronicles centuries of Italian immigration to America which laid the groundwork for the American wine revolution of the 20th century. His new series of mysteries is set in varying regions of Italy, featuring picturesque landscapes, intriguing characters, and the wine, food, and culture of the region. They include *Tuscan Blood, Hunting Truffles*, and *The Secret of Altamura: Nazi Crimes, Italian Treasure.* More on www.DickRosanoBooks.com. His travels have taken him to the wine regions of Europe, South America, and the United States.

In addition to his writing career, Dick has spent many years managing a highly trained team in global nuclear counter-terrorism.

Have you read? More books by Dick Rosano

Tuscan Blood
Tuscan Blood is part mystery, part wine tutorial and part romp through Tuscany's countryside.

Filippo Trantino, the book's narrator, grew up in Tuscany and then moved to America with his family as a child, leaving his heart among the vines of his family's wine estate. He returns home when his nonno, the grandfather he was named for, dies in a freak accident.

Once there, his cousins convince him Nonno Filippo's death was not an accident and that he must investigate it. He promises to do so and while solving the crime, Filippo traverses the pastoral landscapes of Tuscany, indulges in the area's most delicious wine and food and discovers the life he is meant to live.

Hunting Truffles
Northern Italy is the cradle for a precious culinary gem, the white truffle of Piedmont, worth more than gold and sought after by chefs and foodies alike. But this year, the truffle hunters are in a panic as they discover that their usual harvest has been stolen literally from under their feet. Inexplicably, the bodies of murdered hunters turn up, but no truffles. A young man from Tuscany, in tow with his aunt and her restaurant crew, pursue the theft and the thieves through the hills of Piedmont and the wine and food of Italy.

The Secret of Altamura
ISBN: 978-4-86752-311-7

Published by
Next Chapter
1-60-20 Minami-Otsuka
170-0005 Toshima-Ku, Tokyo
+818035793528
27th July 2021

Lightning Source UK Ltd.
Milton Keynes UK
UKHW010958120821
388717UK00001B/123

9 784867 523117